Dark Highways

The Cellar Door Issue #3

Dark Highways

The Cellar Door Issue #3

Edited by Aric Sundquist

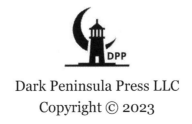

Dark Peninsula Press LLC
Copyright © 2023

Paperback ISBN: 978-1-960788-04-7
Digital ISBN: 978-1-960788-03-0
Library of Congress Control Number: 2023943313

Compiled, edited, and formatted by Aric Sundquist
Cover artwork by Mikio Murakami
Proofread by Elsa Linna and Jen Lammi

Published by:
Dark Peninsula Press LLC
Marquette, MI 49855
www.darkpeninsulapress.com

First Edition.

Table of Contents

Acknowledgments

I would like to say a quick thank you to all the authors in issue #3 who trusted me to edit and showcase their work: Matt Neil Hill, S.R. Miller, Scott McCloskey, Scotty Milder, Christi Nogle, Mary Rajotte, Darren Todd, Charlotte Vale and Mark Wheaton. Also, a huge thank you to Mikio Murakami for his excellent artwork (like always), and to my small band of proofreaders and beta readers: Jen Lammi, Elsa Linna, and Joel Sundquist. And also a special thanks to Daniel Barnett for his keen insight and feedback on choosing stories for this issue.

#

Finally, I would like to say a huge thank you to the featured author of issue #3, Mark Wheaton! Mark first published with Dark Peninsula Press in *Violent Vixens* with his fan-favorite novelette "Killer of Hogs," which also made Ellen Datlow's recommended reading list for 2021. He is the author of numerous novels and novellas, including *Emily Eternal*, *The Quake Cities*, *Who Haunts You*, and has also worked extensively in film and television with Sam Raimi, Michael Bay, and Steven Soderbergh (among many others). I am very pleased to have him return with yet another wonderfully creepy novelette, "Master of the House." Thank you, Mark!

Now, let's begin...

Aric Sundquist
October 2023

Dark Highways

You steer down lightless highways, and you invent a destination because movement is key.

—Nic Pizzolatto, *Galveston*

S.A.L.E.
Darren Todd

To **understand** how it happened, how I ended up staring into the ghastly maw of that one-eyed wretch, you first have to learn a thing or two about yard sales. More specifically, yard sale signs. You've seen them before, even if you've never stopped to browse. Usually poster board, maybe cardboard remnants affixed to telephone poles or stop signs. Scribbled hastily with a black Sharpie.

But like most sub-cultures, they contain a language beneath the obvious. A yard salers' cant, if you will. I had become fluent in this communication over the years preceding that fateful encounter. Not on purpose, but to avoid subterfuge and attend only the best sales on my weekend excursions.

I offer a taste. "Big Sale" usually means it's only big to the person *having* the sale. An unpracticed novice, who believes that a dozen articles of clothing and their old paperback collection justify the adjective "big" when penning their signs.

"Moving sale" has promise, suggesting a certain desperation. But only if the verbiage appears on something temporary. The same assertion on a wooden sign indicates a bait and switch. Perhaps the seller intends to move sometime in the next decade, but you'll not get his wares for anything close to a bargain.

But last year, I spotted a sign that puzzled me. Sure, in hindsight, I wish I'd have given it no more thought than ninety-nine percent of the Arizonans motoring by in the sprawling neighborhoods of Ahwatukee. But it intrigued me. Capital letters on yard sale signs are as common as lower case. But here the word "yard" was lowercase and "sale" was capped and punctuated like it stood for something else: S.A.L.E.

I figured it was a mistake—the sign. Someone genuinely thought that "sale" was an acronym. But so what? Yard sales are a great way to meet people. If you've never lived in a neighborhood with high walls, hot summers, and urban sprawl, perhaps you can't appreciate just how rare it is to speak to your neighbors.

Mistake or not, I had to know. I turned down the road, following the arrow sign at the intersection. The sale looked typical enough: books, clothes, housewares, exercise equipment. A guy in his early thirties was running things, evident by a pleasant smile and his attempt to make eye contact with the handful of people browsing his offerings.

"Morning," I said, raising my mug of coffee in a friendly toast.

"Good morning," he returned. "Can't beat this weather."

He was right. Eight months out of the year, Phoenix was indeed unbeatable. We don't talk about those other four months. We just pay our sky-high electric bills and count the days till fall. But it was May and still temperate. Even odds as Mays go, but it had yet to break triple digits, and the hazy sun and light breeze assured us it wasn't going to today.

"It can stay like this for as long as it likes," I offered. Standard Arizona weather talk.

I browsed the books, mostly pop fic at a buck each. I grabbed a Gaiman hardback, needing a reason to bring up the sign.

"That be all for ya?" the man asked, polite smile in place. "I've got a few Kings in there, too."

I shrugged. "I guess this is it, thanks. Big spender this morning." I held out a single. "Hey, I couldn't help but notice the sign."

The man's demeanor changed. The eager hand that was reaching out to take the dollar now hovered mid-air. His smile froze in place but suddenly looked creepy, failing to match the rest of his body language. He leaned in, still smiling, and whispered, "You have something to say?"

The question hit like a shove to my chest. Not a question, truth be told, but more of a challenge. One I had no desire to answer. I mean, the guy was average height, like me. We were the same age. If anything, judging by a slight paunch at his midsection, I was probably in better shape. But the last thing I'd expected was a physical confrontation.

"No," I told him. "I... I don't."

"Right," he said, and his rigid posture loosened. He plucked the dollar from my hand. "Then have a nice day."

I could have gotten in my car without a scratch on me and only a mildly bruised ego. That could have been the end of it.

But why the flip? I hadn't been in a scuffle since junior year of high school, and that was over whether Larry Andrews had taken one of my horse-piss beers at a friend's house party. Despite social media showcasing guys with frozen-pecker-short fuses fighting over parking spots, adults don't tend to throw hands. Almost never.

By the following morning, I'd started thinking: maybe he wasn't picking a fight. What if he'd been waiting for me to say something... specific? About the sign? Shit, we were talking about the *weather*. By noon, the bee in my bonnet had morphed into a hornet, threatening to bite if I didn't get my ass back to Ahwatukee and find out more.

Even in May, yard sales in the Valley don't often stretch past early afternoon. It might only reach eighty-five degrees at twenty-percent humidity, but when that A-Z sun's hitting you, it can be the middle of January and you just want to get out from under it. But, luckily, by the time I cruised up to the sale at one, it was still going on.

I parked a hundred feet down the road in case he remembered my car; unlikely, since it was the same sun-friendly white as almost every other desert ride. Couldn't wear a jacket; too hot. So I'd opted for a jogging hoodie, one thin as paper and meant more to protect from sun exposure than offer warmth. So, hood up and sunglasses in place, I doubted he could pick me out of a line-up from yesterday.

Even so, what were the odds someone else was going to ask about the sign? It was weird, sure, and certainly yard sales attract plenty of chatty folks, but I instantly felt silly, exposed even. I had every right to be there; he'd invited me onto his property by virtue of the sale. And— having hosted a few sales of my own—I also knew that looky-loos who lingered over wares for sometimes an hour were common. People with nothing better to do or—sometimes—even kleptos looking for the chance to nick DVDs or the like.

But the longer I lurked, browsing the books for the sixth or seventh time, pretending to check my phone over several minutes while pacing the outskirts of the tables, the more I felt—*knew*—I would soon be outed. Either the guy would tell me to leave or worse, discover I was the same person he'd all but called out the day before.

Christ knows how long it'd been, me now baking in the direct sun to avoid the proximity of the carport, despite the blessed shade. Finally good sense overrode my curiosity, and I turned to leave. Only at the edges of my hearing did I catch the question.

"What's with the sign?"

A wave of excitement washed over me. I spun and saw a guy standing under the carport, facing the owner. He was maybe five years younger than me but otherwise indistinct. T-shirt, shorts, flops, phone in hand.

I shuffled closer, whipping out my own phone for cover.

"Something you want to say?" the owner asked, like with me. His posture was hidden from where I stood, but his tone sounded the same. I maneuvered past a lady ogling lamps and moved to the stacks of CDs, well within earshot, even with my back turned.

"Savings. Artifice. Ladybug. Effervescent," the guy said.

What the hell? I risked a look, pivoting with a handful of CDs and peeking with just my eyes, head down.

The owner's gruff exterior—the same look he'd given me— softened at these words. Something else took its place. Not friendly, really. More like... cautious. A little scared, even.

"Right this way," the owner said and turned to enter his house, the other guy following him.

They were inside maybe five minutes before reappearing, the owner affecting small talk about the weather once under the carport. The other guy followed, pulling the door closed behind him with one hand and carrying something in the other. Did he have that on him going in? It was a wooden box—small, rectangular. The glint of brass hinges told me it opened like a jewelry box, but it seemed too shallow to hold a watch. Too wide for a pen set. Cigars, maybe? That still didn't feel right.

They concluded their manufactured conversation, and the visitor told the owner to have a good day. I watched him traverse the driveway, frozen with indecision.

"You a ZZ Top fan?" I heard behind me. I wheeled around to see the owner's smiling face.

He pointed at the CDs in my hands. "Got *Eliminator* in there for sure, but I think I have *Afterburner* in the house. If you're interested."

I thought about that box, about the guy heading to his car and going who knew where with god knows what.

"These are fine," I said and took the top two. I dug into my pants pocket for a couple of bucks. "Thanks."

I speed-walked to my car, keeping the visitor's Celica in my peripheral vision. He was already pulling out as I opened the door and slid inside. But any veteran yard saler knows how to return to the main road almost by instinct, else you find yourself lost in the labyrinthine neighborhoods of Phoenix. So as he rolled out of sight, I took a chance and headed for Southern Avenue, lingering fifty yards from the stop sign, the busy road in sight. A minute later, the Celica showed up. I pantomimed fiddling with something in the passenger seat as he moved past to the intersection.

He headed east, and I quickly followed. He drove just below the speed limit but clearly had no interest in other sales. We passed two neon-yellow signs and he didn't so much as turn his head in their direction. I needed to consider my play. Was I planning on following the guy to his house? Not only was that creepy, what would I say anyway? A yard saler tailing another buyer to ask about something wouldn't be unheard of. We're a competitive, even jealous community.

But the owner's reaction stuck with me. That caution. What was that? Maybe the Celica guy had already paid for whatever that box contained and the seller was suffering remorse, thinking he wanted to keep the thing after all.

Maybe he was scared.

The worry over rolling up into the buyer's driveway vanished when he pulled into a Circle K. Not the gas pumps but into the last shaded spot around the side. I waited by the air compressor for him to go inside. You can tell a lot about people by their walk. I'd picked up on a few tells being a yard saler. I could spot someone in a hurry who wanted to look like they *weren't* in a hurry. Spot the gait of a man pissed off and dying to advertise it, even the slightest swagger of someone who'd pulled one over on a seller: bought a rare item for a song that would fetch a grand on eBay later that afternoon.

But not this guy. He walked like... well, me. Or anyone. Not hurrying, not angry or bitter or even proud.

I jumped out as he entered the glass double doors into the store. Jogged over to his car, heart banging like I'd circled the block at that speed. But what now? I'm gonna break into some dude's car? For the uninitiated, the Phoenix area is great and all, but petty theft is as common as sunshine, so odds were he'd locked his doors anyway, even for a pop-in visit to grab a Coke and some Cornnuts.

I wasn't going to steal anything, just look. See what was in the box and be done with it. And there it lay, on the passenger seat, visible even through the tinted windows. Of course he didn't take it in with him. Why would he? And yet that vindicated me somehow. Spurred me to try the handle. That he'd left the door unlocked only prodded me further. How important could it be, if he'd all but chucked it onto the seat like so much garbage? And everyone knows to lock your doors in Phoenix.

So I ignored my pounding heart, stole a follow-up glance around the corner, and ducked level with the car seat. The interior smelled like vanilla from one of those clip-on air fresheners in the vent. Alongside the box was a *Newsweek*, a half-full tube of Mentos, and a piece of printer paper folded neatly down the middle. I opened it to find a series

14

of addresses, a couple in Phoenix, another in Mesa, and another... the street in Ahwatukee. It had to be the sale we'd just come from.

My tongue went dry, feeling like it belonged to a stranger, like I'd come from the dentist before the Novocain had petered out. I sensed every degree of the sun, the day no longer a kind spring but as if it had ramped up for an early and unforgiving summer. A part of me said to beat feet. Even here, hovering over the seat, if he came back I could bounce up and claim: "This isn't my car!" like some village idiot. But then my hands were on that box, scrabbling at it. I finally saw it had a pendulum clasp, thumbed it, and pried it open.

Inside rested two brass spheres, perfectly round but for a small knob on top. Two empty slots awaited their own spheres. Four slots, four addresses. Two down, I guessed.

But that was as far as I got before my stomach plummeted.

"I thought I had a tail," came a familiar voice behind me, and then a sensation like dendritic fire arced through my back.

I guess I dropped the box, but I wasn't far behind. Only *I* fell to asphalt, the impact masked by the agony in my back. When the shock stopped, I found the wind knocked out of me.

He leaned over me, popping off the wired front from what looked like a gun. He queued an angry arc of electricity at its tip to let me know the taser was still dangerous. "The music fan, right?" he said, grinning. "You'll be okay once you catch your breath, but those prongs are barbed, so be careful taking them out. "I wouldn't suggest following me again. I understand the impulse, honest. But that box... it's not for you, pal. Not today. Probably never."

He dragged me up against the building with surprising strength, as I struggled to breathe. He offered a mock salute, got into his car, and took off. Maybe to fill those other two slots in the wooden box, maybe home, deciding our close encounter was enough for one day.

The shock and the resulting fall had left me exhausted, like I'd barely make it to my car, let alone the drive home. But instead of gratitude—not to the guy, of course, but to... whatever. God, the universe—that I'd made it out intact, a primeval need supplanted any remaining reason. I needed to have that box. Not today, but not never.

#

I spotted no more S.A.L.E. signs that May. None in June, either. I'd asked countless other yard salers whether they'd noticed any odd signs, swapping stories about all the doozies we'd catalogued over time, indulging in the innocent snobbery of any cloistered group. But no luck, and soon the anecdotes lost their humor.

Usually, I'd have given up yard sales for the season by now. Sure, people still hosted them during the grueling summer months, but only before the sun resumed its daily assault. This meant starting at four in the morning. In the world of yard sales, this coupled me with the early birds and furniture hawks—both odd crews, insular and sullen.

I had sketched out S.A.L.E.'s meaning on a Post-it note and affixed it to my dash—an obvious, daily reminder of the unsolved riddle. I felt as if I had a skeleton key with no lock to use it on.

Years before, yard sales had become my *real* work, and crunching data for an insurance company downtown fell a distant second, a mere inconvenience to what I'd rather be doing. But dammit if that wasn't disappearing, and for what? The arcane?

Of course I checked back at the house at Ahwatukee. Most people would host one *maybe* two sales a year, but I figured this guy would prove the exception. Obviously the sale was a front for... well... whatever they were up to. So every weekend, I'd roll by his house. I once saw him taking out his trash, so he still lived there, but no more sales.

Other parts of my life began to suffer. Social life, keeping up with the Diamondbacks, hell, even pleasure reading. I admit I was never the star analyst at work, but now guys I'd once coded circles around were picking up that I seemed... distracted.

It only occurred to me that I hadn't called my own mother for near a month when her name popped up on the car's caller ID. I was out driving, searching. It was Saturday or Sunday. Could have even been a Friday, as desperate as searching out sales on a weekday was. I pulled over and took the call.

"Hey, Mom."

"Now what's the matter? I know that tone."

Two words and she'd outed me. Suddenly I was twenty again, calling from a lonely college dorm across the country, looking for Mom to make it better. The thought made me feel like laughing and crying in equal measure.

I chose to laugh, though the sound came out artificial. "It's nothing. A work... thing."

"Tell me about it."

My mother had spent most of her life raising me and my sister and had since taken up working at a local craft store, no doubt promptly returning most of her paycheck to them in purchases. The thought of her contributing to a discussion of algorithms and embedded if-statements made me chuckle in earnest.

"I know computers," she said, growing defensive, and I actually laughed out loud now.

"Well just talk about it, then, smartypants. Maybe I can't help, but you can talk about it."

I shrugged, though the gesture was invisible to her. She had never attempted to dissemble. Had no desire to pry, so what did it matter if she knew that my problem wasn't really about work?

"I'm trying to find something," I said, finally.

"Okay. Like a new toaster oven?"

"No." I grinned, shaking my head. "A... club, I guess. A secret group."

"And you want to join it?"

I shrugged again and looked to the Post-It note on my dash. "Yeah, I guess so."

She grumbled lightly, a sound I'd heard a thousand times and had learned to identify no matter the volume. "Will they treat you kindly?"

I thought of the look on that Ahwatukee seller's face. It wasn't fear, only caution. Respect, maybe. Then I remembered the buyer, who'd overtaken me with ease. But every group has a pecking order. Not a bad thing. "Yeah, I hope so."

"So why can't you find them?"

"They don't know that I want to join. I think it's like the masons; they have to invite you. Only I can't find them."

"Okay," she said, the word protracted. "How do they find each other? Where do they meet?"

I thought of that list, the addresses. "At yard sales. Ones that a member is putting on."

"So why can't you go, too?"

I shook my head. The large coffee had thinned my patience, and the sun peaking over Camelback Mountain, slapping me in the face, only compounded my souring mood. "There are too many sales. I don't know where to go."

She humphed. "Well... how do *they* know where to go?"

My shoulders slumped, my growing frustration fled. "Hold on. What?"

"If there are too many sales for the other members to find the right ones, then how do they know where to go?"

Of course. It wasn't the signs at all.

"Honey? You still there?"

I chuffed. "It's not a scavenger hunt. Can't be."

"Well I didn't say it was. I was only saying—"

"No, you're right. The guy had a list. They're not just wandering around. The signs aren't the signal. They're talking to each other somehow."

"Sweetie, you're not making any sense."

"Thanks, Mom. You've helped. Really. I have to go." And I ended the call before she'd finished her reply.

"I've been all over," I said to no one now. Two months scouring the valley without finding another S.A.L.E. anywhere. That was too rare.

I drove straight home and searched online for local sales. Not a usual tactic for aficionados, since sales listing anything worthwhile would be picked clean before the sun came up. But I at least knew where to look.

I searched for *S.A.L.E.* on my computer. No dice. Searched "sale" in all caps. A few hits, but they had "yard" capped as well. Maybe they'd put clues in the description. But most write-ups held oodles of details, paragraphs. Made sense: people who took the time to run a classified would practically filibuster to draw more customers.

I asked myself how I'd handle this at work. If you pulled too many records, you either used a better filter or developed a better query. So I copied and pasted the dozens of listings into a single document.

Searched for cigars. Nothing. For pen sets. Nothing. When the answer came, it seemed so obvious, I mentally chided myself.

Savings. Artifice. Ladybug. Effervescent.

Bingo. Three hits, all in the valley. They'd woven the words into the descriptions. "Big savings on all workout equipment" or "make effervescent Italian soda on the cheap" or "collectors item ladybug figurines."

I took a pic of all three addresses with my phone; the closest was only fifteen minutes away, near the university.

My hand wrapped around the front doorknob when the anxiety hit again. *Don't*, it pleaded, inside my head. *Leave it alone.* I felt that lightning searing through my back. The prongs biting into my flesh. He could have caught me on the way down and didn't. He'd wanted me to know what it felt like to eat pavement, to mess in a club to which I had received no invitation. It hurt.

But any group worth joining has an initiation, and I'd paid my dues. It was time to collect.

#

DARREN TODD

The sparse neighborhoods within walking distance to ASU held expensive, dated, tiny houses along streets shaded by high trees. These properties were old enough to have large plots of manicured grass, the cottage-style homes insubstantial, even claustrophobic in the center, set well back from the road.

The yard sale proved easy to spot, with a number of cars lining the street parking, a simple sign and single balloon affixed to the mailbox. Sure enough, the acronym I'd been seeking for so many weekends appeared in trademark black Sharpie. The sight of it alone—S.A.L.E.— threw my heart into overdrive. I was shaking by the time I parked and got out.

The items for sale held no appeal, not only because I was too nervous to even form a mental catalogue of them, but because I was about to join a far smaller circle. I walked to the small poker table behind which sat a man near my age. He held a travel mug, which he raised at my approach.

"Good morning," he said. "Gonna be hot as—"

"I wonder about the sign," I said.

His smile faded, morphed into that caution I'd seen before.

"What's with the spelling?" I asked. "The acronym."

He shifted in his seat, put down his mug, then leaned forward. "Is there something you'd like to say?"

My mouth was cotton, my head so light I had to blink back the white cloud threatening to overtake my vision. I forced a cough and straightened myself. "Savings. Artifice. Ladybug. Effervescent."

The man's mouth hung open for a lengthened second, then he closed it and nodded once. "Right this way," he said and stood. Not even a glance to his other customers, as if whatever they could procure from his wares paled in comparison to what awaited me inside. Only then did I think about money. Jesus, how could I forget to bring cash? I had maybe twenty bucks on me. What if this was not only exclusive but expensive? I'd soon know. I'd found them, passed the phrase. The rest was surely just learning the rules.

20

I followed the guy into his house. The inside telegraphed nothing about his membership, containing the sort of mid-grade furnishings you'd expect from someone this close to the university. Had to have *some* money to afford the real estate but nothing as flashy as North Scottsdale or Fountain Hills. Subtler wealth, like the club.

No one else waited inside, though we passed a greyhound lounging on the couch, seemingly engrossed in the flatscreen TV. The man stopped at a solid-looking door. Brown, suited to the earth-toned paint of the living room walls. Wooden, but obviously sturdy, perhaps with a metal core like the front door. He typed in several numbers on a keypad above the doorknob, conjuring a single beep.

"Just through here," he said and I followed him inside a small, tidy room that might have passed for an office. An old office. No computers or printers, but a roll-top desk, a waist-high file cabinet, and several shelves of books. One shelf of jejune collectibles: a painted plate, a ship in a bottle, a model of the Titanic, a taxidermic fox staged on a fake limb looking down at the Berber carpet.

"So, are you giving or taking?" he asked.

I thought of all the trouble I'd gone through to get here. "Definitely taking."

"All right," the man said, and bent down to a set of small double doors on an antique cabinet. He pulled out a long, wooden case and placed it atop a table between us. "Have a look."

I ran my fingers over the case to find the wood as smooth as marble but for several intricate designs carved into each corner and accented with gold-flake paint. The tight swirls came from no style I recognized, but, complemented by the filigreed brass edges, I'd have guessed Celtic.

The latches sent a last-second spike of adrenaline through me. The same pendulum clasps as the case from the Celica. As my thumbs ran over them now, I imagined the arc of the awful lightning going through my guts, and my core tensed. No matter. I was on his side of the world now. A hunter myself, a collector of....

I opened the case. Sure enough, inside waited at least twenty of the spheres. Nearly all of the circular divots along the felt-lined interior were full of them; only four lay empty.

"Take your time," the man said. "They're not all *my* work, but I'd like to think my contributions stand out."

Like the spheres from the Celica-owner's handheld case, these had small, brass knobs extending out of them. I now knew them to be handles. I pinched one near me between thumb and forefinger and plucked it from the case. As I rotated it upward, my stomach answered in opposite: dropping to the floor and nearly taking me with it.

I was looking at an eye. A human eye, and it was staring back at me, though no longer with any life. Dead, shiny but waxy. I shot a quick glance to the fox, its inert, empty eyes, and instantly understood that what I held in my hand was not a product of taxidermy.

"That's one of mine," the man said. "Note the clarity in the iris. The preserved periorbital veins. Not a single subconjunctival hemorrhage. That takes practice."

I swayed forward, catching myself but then nearly falling back. I replaced the eye with shaking hands and drew another sphere from the box. Again, an eye. Of course, what did I expect? This one blue but foggy and conjuring bile in my throat that forbid me from swallowing.

The man crossed his arms and leaned back, surveying me. "You all right?"

I returned the blue eye to the case, missing the divot two, three, four times before tucking it back in. All I could manage was a rapid nod, my throat too dry to form sounds.

"Good. Well...?"

A new panic set in, realizing that he meant for me to take one. Would that implicate me in a crime? Hell, the guy looked so calm, this could be a sting—a setup to catch these sick fucks at their perverse hobby. He'd think I was one of them, summon the cavalry the moment I'd made my choice. But I *had* no choice: not when facing down the only other possibility: that I was standing in front of a murderer.

I plucked another up, pretended to examine it while fighting back a torrent of acid from my insides, and said only: "This one," the words more a mouse's squeak than human language.

"Not my best piece," he said, shrugging, "but not the worst. 'Course, you didn't exactly pore over them."

I managed a weak laugh.

He shrugged again. "Well. Where's your vessel?"

My breathing shallowed, vision pin-holing. "I... uh...." He must have meant my own box. Like the one the man in the Celica had on his seat. I patted myself down. "I... guess I left it in the car. Lemme go get it."

The man's face changed. His furrowed brow loosened. "Ah," he said, dragging the sound out. "I see. You're not taking. You're giving. Should have known that sooner." He threw up his hands. "Been a little while." He turned, opened a waist-level drawer, and fidgeted with something from inside it.

"No," I said, though the word probably failed to carry even across the small room. "I don't really belong here." I commanded my feet to move toward the door, but my legs felt like they could barely keep me upright. The shoes seemed glued to the floor.

The man turned, and I yelled at his visage, unable to process the round, shiny eyes, the black, protruding snout. Then it registered: a gas mask. The moment I put it together, a cloud of misty, medicinal-smelling gas assaulted me. I shut my eyes reflexively. At last, my feet broke free from the carpet and carried me toward the exit, more stumble than run. With the room's small size, surely it was enough to reach the door. But when I worked the handle up and down, nothing happened. I risked opening my eyes, sure they'd send shards of pain into my head from what I figured was tear gas, only to see that this side held the same touchpad as the outside.

Fate could give me an hour to try the code and still I'd fail; I had paid as little attention to the number sequence as I had every other terrible clue leading me here, every warning my subconscious had tried to impart. I blinked back whatever he'd doused me with, but it wasn't pepper spray. Once again, my vision clouded, slimming into a dot, as if peeking through a keyhole. *Not now*, I thought, but there was no pulling out of it this time. The gas left my eyes unharmed, but it was still doing its work, dragging me under, even as I clawed at the door, shoved my shoulder into it, until I could only slide down to the floor and wait for the black to consume me.

#

I woke to dull pain, blinking over and over as if to clear a foreign object from my eyes, subconscious immediately telling me that something was wrong. We're wired to respond to unknown threats with fight or flight, but once I discovered I couldn't move my arms, the fight part was out. So my flight reflex kicked in, and I bucked as if being cattle prodded, though I quickly found my legs were restrained as well.

I'd been strapped to a table, and I wasn't going anywhere, either. Whatever strength it would take to break those bindings, I didn't possess it. Only after the initial panic dissipated did the *cause* for that panic reveal itself, when my conscious caught up with my subconscious. I was supine, staring up at a dimmed set of adjustable lights, a boring ceiling, the warm glow of a floor lamp in a corner of the small room. But I was seeing all of those through one eye. My other was shut, but not as if crusted in sleep or closed to avoid sunlight. I felt the lid, but it refused to obey my commands to open. But more than that, it felt empty. The skin of the eyelid had—for the entirety of my thirty-four years—held a globe beneath it, one connected to my brain to interpret the world around me. And now it was gone.

A scream followed, though heavily muted by a mask over my nose and mouth. Apparently, it was enough to rouse my tormentor, the yard sale host who'd knocked me out with the spray gas. He came over and examined my face with a small penlight, first my closed eyelid, then my functioning eye, then two thick fingers at my neck to check my pulse.

"I'm going to remove the mask, so you might feel the urge to scream," he said. "I suggest against it. It could make you light-headed and could stress the sutures, as well. Best you stay calm and try to relax. I'll give you an Ativan before you leave, but I'd recommend not taking it until you're done driving."

The whirl of emotions I felt then defies description. First terror, for the missing eye, for still sitting kissing distance from the man who took it, but also trust, even a welcome denial, like he was my doctor and—after a little healing in the safety of my home—I'd get my life back and this could all go behind me. I sat in silence, waffling between this dichotomy of hatred and reverence, of wanting to hurt him and wanting him to assure me that all would be well in time.

His calm, even kind expression suggested that he understood this, though how could he? He still had both of his eyes. "You know, you're pretty lucky," he said. "Well, not lucky absolutely, of course, but lucky relatively. You came to *my* sale."

He leaned in closer, close enough for me to smell a mix of peppermint and coffee on his breath. "I shouldn't say this, but a lot of the others," closer still, "they lack my... precision. Y'see, it takes some real skill to leave the socket intact. For most of the givers, it's an eye patch for life. For you, fortunate, really, you could be fitted with a glass prosthetic eye. That's how," he breathed in deeply through his nose and lifted his chin, "*refined* my work is. I suggest that—all things considered—you remember that fact, reflect on it."

He pulled back, cleared his throat, and rolled his shoulders. "Now, this part is standard fare. Seek us out again, and we'll take other parts from you. Eventually, we'll take everything. So, word of advice, cut your losses... no pun intended. Leave it alone."

He stood, removed my mask, and began loosening my restraints. "That includes the authorities," he said. "You can certainly go directly to the police station. That's your choice, but it won't turn out the way you'd like. What's done is done, if you'll excuse the tautology, and endangering yourself further won't return your eye. That's ours now."

At the final restraint, he turned to gather some papers on a small table, heedless of any threat I possessed. "You may go," he called over his shoulder.

#

The door behind me led to the same hallway we'd taken to enter his office. Just spotting the keypad door made my knees unstable, and I had to catch myself on the wall. The dog looked my way for a moment but showed as little interest in me now as before, when I had been a whole, naive seeker, following its master to the awful culmination of my curiosity.

Outside, the yard sale had ended, only the now-popped carcass of the balloon left dangling from the mailbox. I stumbled to my car a broken man, piloting home a danger to my fellow drivers, swerving and listless. With my remaining eye, I could still see the world, the same colors and signals and occupants, but the handicap now put so many things I'd taken for granted in sharp relief. I had to turn my head farther, felt always as if I would plow into someone if I changed lanes. I missed two turns. But I made it back. I took the pill he'd given me, placing an idiotic trust in this monster who'd deprived me of depth perception, of my ability to drive as thoughtlessly as I once did.

Over the next several weeks, I adjusted to my new life. With seldom a cloud in the sky, I wore sunglasses whenever outdoors, only donning a patch once inside. I looked at glass prosthetics online but the images threw me into a panic, remembering those terrible spheres in the wooden case, the stolen organs of people guilty of only nurturing the same curiosity.

People would ask me about the patch, and I said nothing. Ever. Part of it was my attacker's warning, sure, the other part akin to shame. I considered going to the police, even made it inside the station once. The officer behind the Plexiglas was eating a salad and watching something on his phone. When he noticed me, he paused it, wiped his mouth, and looked up at me from his seat. He took up a dry erase marker and prepared to write on the desk-sized blotter in front of him. "Yessir," he said. "How can I help you today?"

"I... I was just wondering if you could tell me where to find the library."

Even as the officer gave me directions, acid roiled in my gut. Were they watching me now? Did they see where I'd gone, and would they punish me for *almost* seeking justice?

I was a virtual shut-in during the summer months. Not a longshot as Arizonans go. Mostly, I threw myself into work, my one eye perpetually tired from carrying the double burden.

As strange as it sounds, what I missed as much as my eye was going to yard sales. For months, just seeing the signs on the side of the road would send a knife of anxiety into my skull, and I would have to slow my breathing to prevent a full-on panic attack. But after the long summer, those heightened emotions tapered, even as the cardboard notices increased. By fall—a season desert dwellers know may not come until after Halloween—I not only stopped avoiding the signs, I sought them out. Not S.A.L.E.s, of course, but the type I fondly remembered, that I missed. Even after I mustered the courage to stop at one, I acted like a shy dog, wanting the nourishment of his food but only poking at the dish, fretful of the master's hand descending, deserved or not.

Because a part of me worried that the S.A.L.E. people would consider my actions pursuit. That going to yard sales at all constituted further interest in their affairs, deserving of another horrific reprisal. My other eye. My hands, perhaps.

Each weekend of November passed like this. I would drive to sales, peruse their wares, but soon the fear would manifest. Was the man looking at power tools watching me? Was he working with them? What about the woman shadowing the table of cosmetics?

But my endurance dilated with time. By December, I was actually comfortable. No longer some masochistic therapy, the joy returned. I was missing a part of myself, but here —among my people—I would suffer no judgment.

One Saturday found me at a sale way up in Anthem. The sky shone a uniform gray, offering a rare reprieve, so I forewent the sunglasses. I looked up from a table of bric-a-brac to see a man one table over, turned away from me and studying glassware. Surely I noticed the black nylon band across the back of his head. But I ignored any subconscious signals, wondering instead whether this guy really knew his depression glass, a niche I'd indulged in before.

"The lamp might be something," I said softly, so that the owner couldn't hear. Nothing against the fifties man sitting in a folding chair, fingering a tablet. But we buyers shared an invisible bond—friends, even if the sellers were not enemies.

The man seemed to stiffen but didn't respond. I moved to the other side of my table, now within shoulder-tapping distance of him.

"I said, the lamp could be something. Coloration like that. Might be what you're looking for."

At this he turned, closed-mouth smile in place, but he jolted when he spotted my patch, mirroring my own reaction. Another monocular. Another bepatched man.

Even though he seemed like a cat ready to bolt from potential danger, I took the blame. "Sorry," I told him. "Just don't see many patches out there, I guess. I thought about a prosthetic, but... wasn't for me."

My words appeared to offer little comfort. He attempted to reapply his odd smile, but it looked more like his face was being shocked, the muscles moving his lips up into a curl one moment and then falling flat the next. A bead of sweat cascaded down his brow, despite the cool day.

"You all right?" I asked him, my own worry bristling. Plenty of people had only one good eye. There was no reason to think that this man...

But then it flew out of my face without warning. "Savings. Artifice. Ladybug. Effervescent."

The man's face went from discomfort to stark terror, the corners of his mouth turning down, single brown eye going wide, forehead wrinkling.

And then he bolted.

A part of me said to let him go. Another stoked my own fears, like maybe he was one of them. The final part told me to chase him, that I deserved answers. That part held the anger I'd tamped down over the last months, and like water boiling into gas, it expanded, taking up more room than I meant to give it. And so, as quickly as those terrible words had left my lips, my feet were digging into the pavement of the seller's driveway, into the rocks of his yard, and then into the well-watered lawns of a neighborhood park.

Here the man waffled, unsure of where to go. By the time he turned around to look, I was on him, plowing into him more to dispel my momentum than any intention of hurting him.

"I'm sorry," I said, winded. "I didn't mean to knock you down. Just wait a minute."

He struggled beneath me but with no malice, slapping my hands away like a child mounted by a schoolyard bully.

"Calm down," I huffed. "I just want to talk to you."

Our eyes locked, his single brown on my blue, and I knew he was no S.A.L.E. member; he echoed the fear I'd known only weeks before. Had it just happened to him? Was I making it worse? Still, I was sick of unanswered questions, of groping in the dark, of nesting a fear I should never have had to shoulder. The frustration crescendoed, constricting my grip on his hands and upping my voice to a shout.

"Why did this happen?" I said, spittle flying in his face. "Why? Just fucking talk to me!"

He opened his mouth to expose a gaping hole, with only an ugly stump behind his teeth. "'O, 'O, 'O, 'O," he shouted back at me. The N missing, along with his tongue.

LAST FREQUENCY
Mary Rajotte

You know those dead zones where the car radio crackles with static? Where the signal drops away and you swear you hear voices in the ether? They aren't isolated to those lonely stretches of the backwoods, where intermittent flashes of fireflies hint at what goes on beyond the shadows of your high beams. Dead zones linger in other places, too.

It's past the dinner hour. My meter's been running since noon. Not the most exciting way to make a buck, but it lets me go about my business unnoticed. I'm about to call it a night when I get one last airport fare from dispatch. I roll my cab up to the curb and put it in park.

The sun has slipped behind the palm trees, already sinking toward the horizon, so everything shimmers with a dappled glow. The first hint of cool evening air sighs through the half-opened window and sends the delicate chains of various lengths dangling from my rear-view mirror into a mesmerizing dance.

Reaching up, I skim my fingers through my trinkets hanging from the rear-view mirror; a solemn milky moonstone pendant, a tiny pair of bronze wings, and a large silver heart with a smaller heart cut from the center with the word 'Mother' engraved on the front, among other trinkets. They jingle together in a haunting remembrance.

When the back door squeals open, I jump. A blonde co-ed tosses her travel bag into the backseat and then slides in beside it, slamming the door so rough the baubles disrupt my daydream with a discordant tune.

I steal a glance in the rear-view mirror when I splay the chains across my palm to show them off. But time has dimmed their power so much, the passenger doesn't notice. I drop the trinkets to scratch at my stubbled chin and then start the meter.

"Where ya headed?" I ask.

"The River Estates. But I need to make a stop first."

The way her voice breaks at the end, like just being here hurts too much, draws my gaze to her reflection. She checks her watch. Shifts in her seat and tugs at her collar, revealing a small silver pendant at her throat. The music surges on the FM dial, dropping away for a moment before it returns. She glances out the window, cradling a cellophane-wrapped bouquet of pale peonies in her arms. The kind you buy at the corner market from a bucket of stale water. So delicate, so beautiful, but sweating, choking, dying anyway.

Overhead, night approaches. Blue sky has shifted to pink. Seagulls make their nightly sojourn inland. Sunbaked morning glories cool and soften as the daylight dies away. But I don't care about losing light. I'm losing time.

I pull the car into traffic. "This extra stop—"

"I'll direct you," she barks.

"Oh, I'm not worried about that. Just wondering how far out of my way it is. I should have clocked out a half hour ago."

"Look." She reaches for the door handle. Her voice gets higher, her words spilling out so fast she can barely speak. "I'll call another company if that's the problem. You can stop up here and I—"

"Don't you worry. I'll get you where you need to be." I grip the steering wheel and my jaw goes tight. Sundown comes quickly at this time of year. I'll be cutting it close.

"It's Woodward Park." Her words come out thick and choked. "You know it?"

I nod and try to keep the smirk from my lips at how fast my luck has changed. I know it better than she can imagine. It's one of the prettiest little stretches just outside Fresno. My pulse quickens at the thought of being back there. It's like she read my mind. Like just being in the car together puts us on the same wavelength, with the static on the radio as music only the two of us can hear, moving us in an inevitable dance.

Night closes in with a wash of purple that seeps across the radiant horizon. I speed up, chasing down my destination.

"So, you in town for long?" I ask.

"Just a quick visit."

"That's too bad," I say, following the road a while before it peels off north. "It looks real pretty here in the daytime. Sun and big sky as far as the eye can see. Hotter than the hinges of hell in summer, though, if you don't mind the heat."

"You're not wrong. I used to live here."

"Used to, huh? Pity you don't anymore. It's a little slice of paradise. It's why I moved out here from the East Coast. Something about it got under my skin. Good place as any to put down roots, if you ask me."

"Maybe once. A long time ago." She's facing forward, like it's too painful to even look out the window. Her shoulders slump down, like the night pouring in is a cloak too heavy for her to carry.

The city disappears in the rear-view and blackness expands and engulfs us on all sides, tempting my most vile thoughts to prowl all over again. To woo me even deeper, the beginning strums of a mournful little country ditty plays before the frequency evaporates.

"It gets real quiet out here at night," I say, tapping the front of the receiver until it rights itself. "Good thing I've got the voices on this baby to keep me company."

"I'm not much of a talk radio fan."

With a high-pitched whirring, the signal cuts out, and the music gets lost in white noise. A whisper shushes from the speakers. Too quiet for her to hear, but it seeps through the static just for me, bringing goosebumps to my skin.

I find her face in the mirror. Her forehead twitches a moment in half-recognition. It doesn't matter that she's an unwitting witness. She heard the same thing I did, even if she isn't sure what it is.

When the whisper fades and the music comes back, I crank the handle to roll my window down. Night air gusts into the cab, cooling the sweat percolating on my brow. We're getting close. I don't need a map. I feel it in my bones. The voices are willing me to them, and I'm too weak a man to resist.

I snagged my first hitchhiker out here some years back when I was still a long-hauler. Nothing more than a payload to deliver, a stretch of blacktop laid out in front of me like an invitation and a sleeper cab in my rig big enough to hide any manner of sins. The taxi doesn't handle the same way, but it sure blends in easier.

"Is it hard doing what you do?"

I jump when she speaks. Her voice is slow, monotone. So forlorn, it chills my skin.

"Not so much."

"But being out here on your own, you must feel so isolated."

I white knuckle the steering wheel and keep my eyes on the highway. Every time she talks, the radio cuts out, like there's too much energy for the frequency and her voice to share the same space. I strain to hear that dulcet thread coming from the speaker just underneath the melody. "Only for the ones who can't hack that many hours alone."

"And you can?"

I can't help but smile. "Some men are born to live their lives on the road. It's hard not to be seduced by what you can find out here in the dead of night. The views beat anything you'd see at your 9-to-5, I tell ya."

Like a beacon, my headlights illuminate the Woodward Park mile marker ahead. It looms in the distance, a signpost to that moment a few years back—

—when I first spotted the brunette beside her broken-down Jeep in the parking lot where I planned to get a few hours of shut-eye. I downshifted to slow. She leaned against the driver's side door, her arms crossed over her chest, her forehead pulled tight with concern. When she looked up at me in my rig and swept those big curls from her eyes, it was the sweetest sight I ever saw. Her lips weren't moving, but something called out for me—a sweet little voice inviting me to take her. So I did. My last. Until—

"It seems like such a lonesome job," the passenger says, interrupting my daydream. "Driving strangers from one place to another. Only having them in your life for a moment and then they're gone."

"That's why I do whatever it takes to make those moments last."

I skim my hand through the trinkets, the same way the woman absently grazed the half-heart at her throat when I stopped for her that night. The silver heart—*her* heart—twinkles among the others the same way her worry melted into a smile when she looked up at me and chuckled, soft and light. The radio sets off again. Pops and clicks fill the space between sounds. Static fades in and out. Silence. A ghostly breath and then a snatched voice calls out.

Honey?

Crackling. Then white noise.

It's so dark now, only the occasional street light catches the whites of the passenger's eyes. In the mirror, her forehead wrinkles, and her eyebrows pull together with confusion. She heard it. She still doesn't understand, but I do. The static isn't hollow, not to me.

I take the exit and head for the park. I barely pause at the entrance.

"Here's fine," she says as we approach the lake.

I keep going. Away from the main road. Past the parking lots and footpaths. Deeper into the wooded area, where the music goes quiet again, where the trees swallow all sound and in the in-between spaces, the voice comes clearer now.

Honey? Him.

I shift my focus to the mirror. She absently taps the delicate chain, the tiny heart hanging at her throat. My gaze flicks back to the Mother pendant on the rear-view. Two puzzle pieces that fit together. Two broken hearts reunited.

But she doesn't see the other heart. She's too distracted. Too focused on opening her bag to fish out her wallet.

"Stop here," she says, alarm seeping into her voice.

I ignore her plea and follow the gentle curving roadway, chasing the fading signal. It has never been this clear. Not until tonight, when she slipped into my cab. I pound the back of my fist on the dashboard. I need to hear it. Hear that voice. The radio rolls up and down the dial, static intermittently interspersed with speech again.

Serena.

She makes a sound in the backseat.

Serena. Yes.

She lets out a little gasp. So soft, at first I'm sure I imagined it. But when she sits up, her gaze focuses on the dashboard, trying to understand.

I move in front of the radio as though it will block her from hearing. They're mine, these voices. Not for her, even if her being here helps them come through. Accelerating past the sparsely treed embankments, I race through the darkness, taking the sharp turns with targeted control, chasing ghosts that seem too far ahead for me to grasp. They've never been so clear before. Never come unless I'm alone. But with her here, on this night, they're unabashed. And one of them speaks. To her, this time.

Yes, Serena. Him.

She jolts away, as close to the other side of the car as she can, clutching her things in her lap to put distance between us. "Let me out. Now!"

The air grows heavy with expectation. Hers, as she waits for me to comply. Mine, as I wait for the magic of what comes in those empty spaces between the music.

Honey...

She stiffens and edges forward, eyes trained on the dashboard.

"How did you do that?" Her tone is thin and sharper now.

"Sit back."

Serena...

"How do you know my name?"

I reach for the chain dangling from the mirror. "Just sit back!"

Serena. It's him.

"Stop driving! Let me out!"

The voice electrifies my skin the closer we get to where the pavement branches off to the secluded equestrian trails. I squeeze the heart pendant into my palm. I have to hear it again, the voice, that bittersweet sound.

He did this, Serena!

Shivers surge up my arms, spider web across my shoulders, my neck. The words are distinct now. Clearer than they've ever been. As clear as she sounded that night out here, where it happened.

Him!

From the backseat, Serena forces herself between the seats and lunges for the pendant hanging from the mirror, but I grip it tight and swerve the car onto the grass, where we skid to a stop.

"How did you get this?" she shouts.

She grabs the chain. Yanks it until it breaks. I spin to face her. The heart scratches my palm as she pulls it free. She's holding it in her closed hand, dangling it next to the one around her neck. They match.

"What the hell did you do? What did you do to her?"

I spin my arm in an arc, swiping the air to take the necklace back, but the radio hisses and then a warbling trill comes through.

Serena, yes. Honey. Him.

She fumbles for the door handle but misses. When more voices cry out, she stops.

...was you...

...did this to me...

...murderer...

Her tear-filled gaze flits from me to the baubles and then back again. "You... killed all of them, too. *Didn't you?!*"

The display blazes bright neon and the dial moves through all the stations until it goes dark and the static cuts to silence. There's no more music. No soothing sounds. Instead, from the station, countless voices cry out. One after the other, they each give their testimony until they overlap and intertwine in a dizzying refrain of my secrets, revealed.

...you murderer...

...disgusting...

...never again...

...make you pay...

The back of my neck seizes with a frigid intensity that surges to my temples. I smash my fist on the radio until the knobs fall to the floor and the plastic display cracks. The music is gone now, but the voices still come. Angry this time instead of fearful like they've always been, like they were when I took them. When the signal dies out, they come back anyway. Not from the speakers, but from all around me.

—vile... disgusting... shame... murderer—

When Serena kicks my seat, I'm jolted from the accusations, but she's out before I can stop her. She bounds around the front of the car, heading for that place where my past lies buried with hers. Sobbing, she falls to her knees, where a time-shriveled bouquet sits propped against a sycamore tree in memoriam, a keepsake that only makes sense to someone who knows what happened here, knows what was lost, what I took.

I bolt from the car and chase after her, but she's back up on her feet, screaming and running toward the main road before I can subdue her. Around me, the discord, the cries, the static and sounds all clamor together.

My screams can't drown them out, so I dig my fingernails into my temples to drag the voices free somehow, but it does nothing. All I ever wanted was to find that ideal time and place to hear them and sate my hunger so it wouldn't grow any further. Somehow, having her here gave them the power they needed to keep them from fading. But instead of those delectable little whispers I love to savor, they blurt out my secrets, no longer restrained to those empty spaces between sounds, or to those shadowed places where I hoped they would stay entombed forever.

With every uttered syllable, their souls punish me.

They lash out, afflicting my arms with deep wounds. Their screeches ravage my eardrums until they bleed. A surging wave whips me with tornadic rage, abrading my eyes, blinding me, forcing me to my knees in endless darkness. All around me, the voices of my victims resonate in an endless echo of their vengeance personified, their collective rage resurging, unloosed in one last frequency.

TWELVE MILES.
TWO HOURS.
Scotty Milder

"**H**ot damn."

Ben sounded choked, like his throat had suddenly filled with cement.

Christa didn't respond. She didn't dare take her eyes off the road. Her jaw hurt from clenching, and the hands gripping the steering wheel had gone slippery at the palms and white at the knuckles.

"Wow," Ben said. "Just... woweee wow."

Christa wanted to scream at him to shut up, but was concerned even that momentary lapse of concentration would lead to a chain reaction terminating in a thousand-foot plunge and their own mangled, fiery end.

Fuck, she thought, her mind buzzing with a terror so crystalline it morphed into a euphoric sense of astonishment. *We might actually die this time.*

\#

"Don't worry," she'd said gamely as they left their apartment in Colorado Springs a week ago. "I can handle it."

And she could. She was sure of it.

Well... pretty sure. The plan was to save Black Bear for the end—either as a grand, triumphant finale or a finale of another, more tragic kind. They went over Engineer Pass first three days ago, and that was a breeze: a gentle ascent into clouds and postcard-ready views of distant, snow-capped peaks. Yesterday's trek up Imogene Pass was a fair amount spookier, mostly because they came upon an old Willys descending at the absolute worst possible moment, where the "road" (such as it was) narrowed down to a slick-rock shelf and curved beneath a waterfall. A hundred feet of vertical cliff rose on their left. On their right: a drop-off into absolute nullity. She'd had to very carefully back down the road to find the narrowest of turnouts.

That was a rough fifteen minutes, but it was well within her Jeep-trailing skill set. Her dad had made sure of that. The Saturday after she got her license, he woke her up early and steered them east out of Vail, then made her swap with him in Silverthorne so she could drive over Loveland, which was the highest paved mountain pass in the lower forty-eight states. It was also—with its blind turns and almost mocking lack of guard rails—scary as shit on the way down. Especially for a sixteen-year-old girl who'd been making learner's-permit grocery runs with her mom less than a week before.

After they got to the bottom, Dad directed her back up I-70 to the Starbucks in Silverthorne. It wasn't even noon yet. He took her inside and bought her a hot chocolate.

"So? What did you think, Squirt?" he asked.

"I hated it."

He took a swig off his latté. His eyes were severe, but a laugh danced within them.

"Okay. But you kind of loved it a little too. Right?"

She hesitated, trying to decide if she should answer truthfully or not.

"Yeah," she finally agreed, her own grin threatening to surface. "I guess I did."

She'd done Engineer a dozen times in the years since, and Phantom Canyon and Argentine Pass at least that many. She'd gone through the Gold Belt Byway eight times, the Oh-My-God Road six, up Imogene four times, and down the dreaded Schofield Pass between Marble and Crested Butte once. There was the Steel Bender and Hell's Revenge over in Moab (two times), Apache Trail down by Phoenix (four times), Miller Canyon in California and Red River in New Mexico (once each). And there were the dozens upon dozens of unmarked forest roads, canyon roads, shelf roads, and rock crawls throughout the San Juans, the Wasatch, the Sierras, and the Gila.

Ben started to come along once they started dating. He brought his fancy cameras and his drone after the first couple of trips. After a few more he began bugging her to start a YouTube channel. She finally agreed. So here they were.

The channel was going to be called *Boondockin' with Christa and Ben*. "Boondockin'" had been her dad's word. And after years of doing it herself, these roads were to her like a football in the hands of Tom Brady, or a Louisville Slugger to Aaron Judge. An extension of herself in a primordial way she couldn't quite explain.

Black Bear, though... this road was something else entirely. It was Mount Everest for Colorado Jeep-trailers, the Final Fucking Boss, the singular beast that had to be defeated. Schofield was technically deadlier, but Black Bear had the majesty that came with enormous—indeed, almost incomprehensible—height. Even though she'd done nearby Imogene enough times to be an old hand at it, Christa had somehow never found the balls to take on Black Bear.

She and Ben had rolled into Telluride two days ago. They got out, wandered all the little shops and boutiques on West Colorado Avenue for a while, and finally gazed up at the switchbacks: a descending ladder zig-zagging crazily down the pyramidal cliff just west of town. Ben turned to her, his grin wicked, and said, "It ain't too late to back out, you know. I won't lose respect for you."

Those were the magic words. He might as well have waved a red flag in front of a bull.

So they'd set out at just after seven that morning, grabbing a couple breakfast burritos at a little coffee shop on Ouray's nearly deserted main street. As they ascended out of the sleepy village, the familiar butterflies began to tickle the inside of Christa's ribcage. She felt sick and shaky from adrenaline, but her mind focused down to a singular, knife-edge point. At the tip of that point was a searing, bone-deep pleasure that was better than love, better than food, better than sex. It was one step away from religious epiphany. She knew once she was up there and dangling off the edge of everything, she'd never want to leave.

A few miles up the highway, the old wooden sign pointed back toward the mountains and gave its jaunty warning: "TELLURIDE——> CITY OF GOLD, 12 MILES - 2 HOURS. YOU DON'T HAVE TO BE CRAZY TO DRIVE THIS ROAD BUT IT HELPS! JEEPS ONLY."

It didn't quite say "*fuck around and find out*," but it may as well have.

They'd fucked around.

And now Christa was finding out.

#

"Wow," Ben said again.

She gave in. "*What?*"

"It's just... look at that view," Ben was saying.

"I'm a little busy making sure we don't roll off the side of the goddamned—"

"So *stop* a minute. It's not like there's anyone behind us."

Fair point. She tapped the brake lightly, easing the Jeep to a creaking halt. She pulled the emergency brake and shut the engine off. They sat there for a moment, listening to the *tick-tick-tick* of the motor cooling down. The smell of gas, dust, and scorched brake pads hung thick in the air.

"Want to stretch your legs?" Ben asked. "I wouldn't mind grabbing a couple shots."

"Sure," Christa said. She glanced past Ben out the passenger window, which showed nothing but a perfect rectangle of sky. "Can you get out?"

Ben rolled down the passenger window and poked his head out.

"Uh," he said, sounding a little sick. "No."

She glanced out her own window. The jagged cliff looked close enough to touch, but she thought she had a couple feet to squeeze out.

"All right," she said. "Just be sure not to kick the parking brake when you climb over."

"Yes ma'am."

He leaned over to check the dashboard camera. She squeezed out and wriggled her way to the front of the Jeep.

The door banged and scraped against rock behind her. Ben cursed.

"Don't fuck up my Jeep!" she yelled.

He muttered under his breath. She smirked and gazed into the valley.

He was right. The view was breathtaking. She knew, from all the trail guides, that the excruciatingly tight turn at the end of the first switchback was nine-hundred feet above the valley floor. They were now on the third switchback, which shaved maybe a hundred feet off that number. Still plenty high.

The pine-studded mountains funneled perfectly into the narrow, green valley below. Telluride sprawled across the bottom like a cow lazing in the sun. Bridal Veil Falls thundered down the rocks to her left.

She shuffled up to the rocky ledge and looked over. There were nine more switchbacks to go. She could see each of them, twisting down the cliff like a crazy Escher drawing.

Ben crunched up next to her. "Jesus, look at that," he said.

She turned, expecting to see him peering into the valley, his eyes inevitably (and sexily) narrowed as he planned his shots. But he was looking back at the Jeep. She followed his gaze and saw the front tire pooching off the edge.

"Yep," she said. "My dad warned me. This road isn't kidding."

"It sure as fuck isn't." Ben turned back to her and winked. "But I got faith in you, babycakes."

"Ugh," she said, but let him kiss her anyway. That was their game; he called her "babycakes" to get a rise out of her, and she pretended to be annoyed. He pulled away and finally looked out into the valley. Those dark eyes narrowed, and she melted inside—a normal response to his gaze. She glanced past his shoulder and saw the drone sitting on the Jeep's hood.

"You think I got time to grab a few shots?" he asked.

An engine rumbled above them. She looked up and saw a metallic glint moving along the first switchback. There had been a blue Rubicon Jeep coming up behind them. This must be them.

The glint inched along. Whoever was behind the wheel was not confident.

"Unless they speed up, you've got at least a half hour before they make it down to us," she said.

"*Sweet,*" he said, and turned to the drone. He fiddled with it and, seconds later, it was buzzing up the cliff face.

"Keep it away from them," she said uneasily. "Last thing they need is you startling them with that thing."

"Good point," he said. His thumbs worked the joystick and the drone shot out over the valley.

"Wave hello to your future fans!"

She waved and watched the drone disappear into the blue, dwindling down to a black dot before being swallowed by the sun.

Dad would have loved this, Christa thought, and felt that familiar fist wrap around her heart. Her vision prismed. She swallowed thickly and wiped her eyes with the back of her hand.

Meanwhile, the Rubicon crawled along the cliff above them.

#

Ben hopped out at the end of the switchback and spotted Christa around a harrowing four-point turn. He climbed back in and they kept going, crunching precariously over rocks and banging through divots. The Jeep tilted crazily toward the void. She kept her eyes trained to the shelf before her; the vast emptiness of sky out the driver's side window pressed in like a weight.

"This one seems like it's not so bad," Ben said.

He was right. The road, while no less rough, was perceptibly—if nanoscopically—wider. The rock-strewn slope on their right seemed a bit less severe. And the pines were creeping back in, making the landscape feel a bit less alien.

"Dad always said this is where things get the most dangerous. When you start relaxing." Christa said.

"Still. Better than the last one."

"Yeah." She grinned. "You doing okay over there?"

"Yep. I trust you, babycakes. Never doubted you for a second." He waved at the dashboard camera. "So, for all our loyal viewers—was Black Bear everything you dreamed it would be?"

"Ask me again when we're at the bottom," Christa said. "We've still got eight switchbacks to go."

"Jesus Christ. Really?"

"Everyone says the first three are the worst," she said. "But I'm not going to get cocky about—"

"*LOOK OUT!*"

She jammed her foot on the brake, all her father's training slurping out of her. The Jeep groaned in protest and for one terrible second it skidded to their left, where the road fell away and the sky swallowed everything.

At the same time, Christa saw a flutter of movement overhead. A rotating shadow tumbled down the cliff toward them. She could hear the bang and scrape of metal against rock.

Then the Rubicon slammed, canopy first, to the road maybe ten feet in front of them; if Ben hadn't seen it coming, they would have been pancaked.

It didn't look much like a Rubicon anymore; Christa vaguely recognized the shattered black spaces where headlights used to be, the twisted chrome snarl that had been the grill. The rest was crumpled metal and a hint of shredded tires flapping crazily like vultures' wings.

All of it enshrouded in a swirling cloak of dust.

It was there for a half-second that felt like a year—long enough for the image to burn itself into Christa's mind. And then the momentum carried it over the edge and it was gone.

They stared through the windshield, dumbfounded. Christa's mind screamed at her, tried to proclaim she'd imagined it, that it couldn't have *really* happened, not *really,* no fucking way, right? *Right*?

As they watched, a silvery plastic hubcap fluttered down and landed gently on a clump of scrub oak.

"Holy fuck," Ben breathed. "Holy, holy, holy fuck."

"Get out," Christa said.

Ben gaped stupidly at her. His face had gone white, tinged with a shade of green.

"*Get out,*" she repeated. Her voice vibrated like a reed. "I don't have room on my side. We need to see... if there's anyone..."

He swallowed, throat clicking, and fumbled for the door.

#

Once they were outside, the Rubicon's path down the cliff was obvious. Christa could see the spot on the second switchback where the vehicle crept too close to the edge and a chunk of granite crumbled away beneath it. From there: a linear, whitish scar down the slope, speckled here and there with pieces of metal and twinkling shards of glass. A stumpy pine was snapped off at mid-trunk.

She went to the other edge and looked down. The Rubicon had vanished into the pines below, but its path of destruction was even more obvious over here: trees gouged and broken, great white rips torn into the rock. Deep in the green canopy of pines she saw a glint that might have been the remains of the Rubicon, or at least a fair-sized piece of it. She counted; if that was it, it hadn't stopped until just above the ninth switchback. A six, maybe seven-hundred-foot plummet.

"There's no way anyone survived that," Ben said beside her.

As if in response to that, someone up above started screaming.

#

Christa was pretty sure it was a woman. But the shattered agony in that voice made it impossible to tell for sure.

There were no words, or at least none Christa could discern. Just a hollow, formless shrieking that went on, and on, and *on*...

They both checked their phones and were unsurprised to find that neither of them had any reception. Ben tried the CB mounted under the dash, but was answered only with the unforgiving hiss of static. He didn't even bother with Christa's GMRS; the unit absolutely flummoxed him.

"What do we do?" he asked after giving up.

"One of use should go up there," Christa said. "The other should stay here and keep trying the CB."

"What do they do if someone saw the crash from below?"

"I think they'll probably close the pass at both ends and send up search and rescue from below. An ambulance, maybe. Or maybe a helicopter. I don't know."

Ben looked back up the cliff, where the screaming had—for the moment—abated.

"I'll go up," he said. "I got a first aid certification five years ago. It's long lapsed, but I think I remember most of it."

"Okay. I'll move the Jeep down to the end of the switchback. Hopefully there'll be enough room for me to pull off and let emergency vehicles squeeze through."

He nodded. "Maybe whoever it is up there already died—"

On cue, the screaming started again. Only this time, it sounded more like sobs. *Definitely a woman*, Christa thought.

Christa started to edge her way around the Jeep to climb back in.

"Hold up," Ben said, and opened the back. He rooted around for a

49

couple minutes. Christa heard the bang and thud of various Pelican cases.

Don't take a camera, she thought, dismayed.

But instead, he pulled out his rolled-up sleeping back, a cylindrical container filled with bungee cords, and two long pieces of black metal that she recognized as the strut poles for his camera jib.

He caught her gaze and blushed, unaccountably embarrassed.

"It's probably stupid," he said. "I figured maybe I could make some sort of litter. Worst comes to worst, maybe I can drag them down to you."

She went on her tiptoes, kissed him fully. "It's not stupid at all," she said. "Once I get the Jeep down to the end, I'll walk back up here and holler up at you. Okay?"

"Sounds good," he said. He flashed a heroic grin, slung the struts over his shoulder, and started hiking up the road.

She watched him for a moment, thinking *if we get out of this without things getting too bloody, you may get lucky later.* There was that melty feeling again, all squishy and warm, but it curdled when the sobbing above cycled into shrieks.

Get going, she barked at herself, and climbed into the Jeep.

#

Luckily, the end of this switchback was wider than the last, and had a pretty long turnoff where she could park the Jeep and leave just enough room for an ambulance (a small one) to make the hairpin turn.

She parked the Jeep and turned on the CB. There were a few pops and crackles behind the static hiss, and strange whale-song murmurings that might have been buried voices. She imagined truckers trundling up the Million Dollar Highway, asking each other the best place to get a burger in Durango.

She raised the handset to her lips. "Breaker breaker, my name is Christa Stuart and I've got a 10-34 *emergency emergency S.O.S.* on the Black Bear switchbacks. A vehicle has gone over the side, and we think there's at least one survivor near the top. If you can hear this, please relay this information to emergency services in Telluride. Over."

She listened. More cracks and pops. Something that could have been a throaty chuckle.

She turned to the GMRS, which was mounted on the dash just below Ben's camera. She turned it on, and was disquieted by the absolute nothing coming through the speakers. There wasn't even an electrical hum.

"Hello, this is call-sign KQVAOB, Christa Stuart. I'm reporting an accident on the Black Bear switchbacks. A vehicle has gone over the side. There may be survivors. Please relay this information to emergency services in Telluride. *S.O.S. emergency emergency.*"

She listened. Nothing.

Her dad spoke up from the back of her mind: *you know those damn things are useless for emergencies, Squirt. How many times did I tell you that?*

"I know," she said.

Why didn't you get the satellite phone like I told you to?

"Too expensive," she said.

Dad didn't have an answer for that, but she could imagine the haughty sneer that would be creeping across his lips by now. He'd shake his head and walk away with a rueful chuckle. Then a week later her inbox would be flooded with links to satellite phones and whatever online coupons he could find.

Fat lot of good the satellite phone did you anyway, she thought before she could stop herself. *Didn't stop you from—*

Christa choked that off. If you were to ask her whether she was angry at how her father died, her face would turn to stone and she'd growl *of COURSE not!* But maybe you'd see a different truth lurking in her eyes. After all his training and all his harping at her about what model of Jeep to buy, what kind of tires were best, even the best brand of sleeping bag to carry in case of an emergency, he'd ended his days by falling asleep after a couple beers at the roadhouse and slamming his pickup into a utility pole four blocks from his house.

He and Mom had just retired down to Mesa six months earlier. He was building a patio. Christa had talked to him on the phone about their dream vacation—to Bolivia, where they'd mountain-bike down the old Yungas Death Road—just the night before.

The man had tackled Hell's Revenge *seven times*. He'd rolled his own Jeep twice and walked away with nothing but a couple scrapes and a belly laugh. How could he possibly die so stupid?

She grabbed the CB handset again.

"Breaker breaker, my name is Christa Stuart and I've got a 10-34 *emergency emergency S.O.S.* on the Black Bear switchbacks. Please come back. *Over."*

Crackle.

Pop.

Murmur.

"Breaker breaker, my name is Christa Stuart and I've got a 10-34 *emergency emergency S.O.S.* on the Black Bear switchbacks. *Please* come back! *Over!"*

Crackle.

Pop.

Then a garbled stream of syllables, mostly buried in static. The voice was low and decidedly male, but the interference made it sound odd and robotic. The words were in no language she recognized.

"Breaker breaker! My name is Christa Stuart and I've got a 10-34 *emergency emergency S.O.S.* on the Black Bear switchbacks. *COME BACK. Over!"*

Crackle.

Pop.

Then a single garbled word.

It sounded like "kathartirio."

She raised the handset to her mouth. Stopped. The day was hot, even up here at twelve thousand feet. But a chill settled into her nonetheless.

That voice.

She didn't know how she knew it, but it wasn't the voice of someone who was likely to help. She tried to picture the face that went with it, and all she could dredge up was a lumpy, tumorous darkness in the rough shape of a man.

She hung the handset back on its hook and climbed out of the Jeep. She rubbed her arms, which had inexplicably popped out in rails of gooseflesh, and looked down at Telluride. It was the middle of the day, but the town seemed to be sleeping blissfully. As still as a painting.

A thought tumbled into her head, as if pushed in from the outside: *That town is deserted.*

Her breath locked in her throat. She turned and looked back up the switchback, hoping to see Ben huffing his way down, the injured person strapped into the makeshift gurney behind him. But there was nothing but the gentle sway of stunted pines in the lightest breeze. And it occurred to Christa that the screaming had stopped altogether.

She trudged back up to where the Rubicon had gone over. She craned her neck and looked up.

There was someone up there. A shadow flitting busily against the cliff face.

"BEN!" she yelled. *"WHAT'S GOING ON? ARE YOU OKAY?"*

Her voice ricocheted off the cliffs like a bullet. The last syllable— *"KAY... KAY... kay... kay..."*—drifted away like an untethered balloon.

The shadow stopped moving. She felt eyes pressing down on her, and felt the inexplicable urge to turn away.

She waited for Ben to shout back down to her.

He didn't.

#

Christa wasn't sure how many hours had passed. She kept going back and forth between the Jeep and the crash site, waiting.

At the Jeep, she methodically scanned through all the channels on both the CB and the GMRS, always shouting the same message: *emergency emergency S.O.S... there was an accident on Black Bear Pass... a vehicle went over the edge... please send someone.*

The GMRS stayed silent. The CB continued to spit noise. Once or twice she thought she heard that awful voice again, but it was immediately subsumed in an oscillating wave of static.

Back at the impact site, she continued to call up to Ben. Once, she thought she heard a gasp. Another time, there was a chunky, ragged sound that may have been heavy breathing. After that came a low rustle that could have been fabric; she hoped that meant he was up there with the sleeping bag, easing the injured person into the makeshift chamois. But he never called back down. She craned her neck, hoping to see him. But there was nothing.

That undulating shadow, whatever it was, was gone.

After a while she simply sat on the edge of the road, letting her legs dangle into the abyss and staring out at the silent town below. They weren't so far away that she shouldn't be able to see the ant-like movement of cars on the wide, grid-like streets. But it was like Telluride had emptied out; it made her think of the model towns she saw in those PBS documentaries about nuclear tests. She half expected to see a mushroom cloud split the horizon, followed by the booming rumble of the shockwave rolling toward her.

The unpaved farm and county roads closer to the pass were equally lifeless. There was a colorless old pickup truck parked cockeyed along the shoulder of a straight dirt track near the mountain's base. It was the only vehicle in sight, and had been sitting abandoned for hours.

Speaking of...

She twisted around and looked back up. The switchbacks were as apparently empty as the town below. And that made no goddamned sense at all, because—with its fearsome reputation and the short window without snow—you could count on the switchbacks being choked with thrill-seekers all the way down. It was catnip to off-roaders and weekend warriors. She and Ben had left early in the hopes of avoiding the crush, and they'd lucked out; by the time they got to the infamous Steps immediately above the switchbacks, it was just them and the Rubicon trundling behind them. But it was midday now, and the pass was still empty. *Someone* should have come along by now.

"*Ben!*" She yelled. Her voice was hoarse, and it didn't carry very far.

Forget the CB and go up there. Figure out what the fuck is going on.

It wasn't the first time she'd had the thought. But, for whatever reason, every time she resolved to do just that a frosty corkscrew of unease twisted into her spine. She'd take a few steps up the road and stop. She'd hear a low, wolfish voice in the back of her head—*kathartirio*—and the muscles in her legs would seize up tight.

So she sat. And she waited. The switchbacks faced Telluride from almost due east, and she had an almost perfect view of the sun as it reddened slowly like a boil and dropped toward the mountains. Eventually it touched the snow-capped summit of one of the peaks and golden rays spoked out from it into the cloudless blue.

Dad now:

I think you may be a little bit fucked, Squirt.

Right on the heels of that, something rustled against the rocks overhead. The gasp was undeniable now, but it wasn't pain or fear. It was like someone in the grip of an orgasm.

She looked.

The shadow was back. Man-shaped and lurking at the edge of the road. Perfectly still. She couldn't see a face, but she knew it was watching her.

Something shot past it and plunged sharply down. Whatever it was dropped in front of the descending sun; it took her just a second to recognize that it was Ben.

He was silhouetted against the dying light, so she couldn't see his face. But she was certain that he was smiling.

And then he was gone.

The thud came seconds later.

She clapped a horrified hand to her mouth. A chirping whimper escaped her, and she felt a scream trying to push up from beneath it.

Don't look, she thought. *Don't look don't look don't look—*

But of course she did.

And the scream, when it came, seemed to go on forever.

#

Scrape...

Christa snapped awake out of a broken dream filled with screaming metal and crimson fountains of blood. For a moment she was twelve again, camped out in her family's back yard in Vail, staring up at the stars from the cocoon of her sleeping bag.

But these stars were different; tactile shards of hardened light chipping out of the perfect velvet black of the night. It was like she could reach up and run her hands across them, feel their gemstone toughness beneath her fingers.

These were mountain stars.

It all slammed back into place: the Rubicon, the screaming, the strange voice on the CB, Ben's blissful leap into the etherea of encroaching twilight, followed by his prosaic and pulverized end on the fifth switchback below: face down in an expanding lake of blood, his limbs and spine bent at impossible angles.

Christa forced herself to sit up. The muscles in her neck and lower back shrieked. She was still on the fourth switchback, nestled into the lumpy cleft between road and cliff face. After the thudding completion of Ben's rapturous plunge, she had crawled mewling from the edge, wormed across the road, and pressed herself as deep into the cliff as she could. Her mind chattered a single word, over and over again:

No... no... no... no...

At some point she fell asleep again. And now night had fallen.

The air was still and cool. There was no wind, and the silence had a completeness that felt physical.

Scrape.

Christa peered up the road, to where the switchback ascended into darkness.

Something was coming.

She lurched to her feet, stumbled into the middle of the road, and looked down to where the lights of Telluride should have been twinkling. The blackness was complete and unbroken. She thought this must be what it felt like to be an asteroid or a comet out in the Oort cloud somewhere, hurtling endlessly through the dense opacity of space.

A woman staggered out of the gloom and weaved drunkenly toward her. She was moving slowly, each quivering step a plodding uncertainty. Christa waited for her to tumble off the edge.

She didn't. As she got closer, Christa could see that she was wearing a pair of denim shorts that clung to long legs that would have been shapely and inviting if they didn't have a few too many jagged bends in them. Her feet were clad in an expensive pair of tennis shoes; one faced forward, and the other was twisted ninety degrees inward. Her tank top had at one time been light colored, but now it was Rorschach-spattered with blood that went black against the night.

The woman's right arm was gone at the shoulder. Ragged clumps of muscle and sinew jutted from the hole like sea-slickened ropes of kelp. The other hung useless, tick-tocking metronomically with each lumbering step.

Christa flashed back on any of a dozen zombie movies she and Ben had watched together. Except this woman couldn't be a zombie, because even a zombie couldn't survive what had happened to her head. The left half of her face looked fine, and Christa could see that she had been youngish and pretty, with full lips and sharp supermodel cheekbones. The hair that remained on that side was long and dark and luscious.

The right half of her face was a misshapen pit: a red mass of quivering tissue rimmed by sharp wedges of bone. There was fluffy,

57

pinkish tissue inside there that Christa knew was what was left of the woman's brain. It had been pulped into something that looked like tapioca pudding sprayed out of an uncovered blender. Her jawbone was entirely exposed, and what few teeth were left were hopelessly shattered.

As the woman closed the distance, Christa could hear her muttering:

"Where are we? Where ARE we? Where... are we?"

Twenty feet away now.

"Where *are* we?"

Ten.

The single roving eye found Christa in the starlight. The remaining half of her mouth twitched into a wobbly smile.

"Where are we?"

Christa thought about the voice on the CB, the word, the perfect blackness of the valley below.

"I don't know," she said.

The woman nodded (or maybe her head just bobbed inanely on the shredded coil of exposed muscle) and stumbled past.

"Where are we?" she asked nobody as she descended toward the Jeep. "Where *ARE* we?"

Through the radio, that strange word echoed again, as if answering her desperate pleas:

Kathartirio.

But this time—the voice sounded like her father's.

Christa watched the darkness swallow her. She could hear the woman's murmurings for another minute or two, and then the silence closed back around her.

From behind her:

Scrape.

The light scatter of pebbles.

Something else was coming.

Christa closed her eyes. Her mind went back to her dream from before—which maybe wasn't a dream after all. There were only a few scattered images and sensations: something slamming into them from above, the world suddenly tilting crazily, Ben getting yanked out of the open passenger door as if on a string. The scream of metal against rock. Something (Ben again?) twirling off into the blue. And then the sensation of falling...

falling...

falling...

...and watching the ground rush up to meet her.

Scrape.

Christa's eye snapped open. She thought she should probably turn around. Get herself ready. But she didn't. She knew who it was. Or who it used to be. She could imagine his smile, so easy and vaguely, adorably condescending behind the flash of perfect white dentures. There'd be a mirthful twinkle in his eyes. *How're you doing, Squirt?* he'd ask in that warm blanket of his familiar voice.

Except that was wrong. The voice wouldn't be warm. It would be the reptilian rumble from the CB. And even if he called her Squirt and asked her how she was doing, that word—*kathartirio*—would lurk behind every syllable.

How're you doing, Squirt?

(kathartirio)

Fancy meeting you way up here!

(kathartirio)

You're early. I thought it would be awhile before I saw you again.

(kathartirio)

And there'd be no twinkle in his eyes. They'd be as black and depthless as the yawning valley. Because whatever happens after you slam your truck into a utility pole and break your neck changes you. Something drains away. And something else comes in.

It was happening to that woman. It had already happened to Ben.

It was going to happen to her, too.

Scrape.

Maybe a hundred yards back, getting closer. She kept her eyes closed, breathed in the mountain air. She could follow the woman, put distance between herself and the shadow behind her. But why bother? It would catch up to her eventually.

Scrape.

The face might look familiar, or it might not, but either way once she saw it she knew she would scream and she would try to run away. Because once she peered into those black eyes, she would finally know what the word meant. Everything it implied. And something essential would snap off in her mind and spin out into the darkness.

Kathartirio.

She murmured to herself, and her own voice grated against her eardrums like sandpaper: "I can handle it."

And she could. She was sure of it. She started repeating the words over and over, like a mantra: "I can handle it, I can handle it…"

Well…

Scrape.

Pretty sure.

LIGHTS OUT, EVERYTHING OFF

Christi Nogle

Sweetie was the solution that Linda and others like her had prayed for over the years. She was a cross between a fifties Cadillac and a sixties Microbus, but roomier, sleeker. Her exterior was raspberry, white, and chrome. Her interior was sparkly vinyl, witty boomerang-patterned Formica, and maple veneer. Linda had decorated with pretty cushions and blankets and dangling herbs and houseplants. Sweetie's solar-charged electric battery ran her lights and devices. A rain-collection system and latrine-digger made Sweetie self-sustaining in a pinch whenever Linda couldn't hook up, but usually there were hook-ups. Everyone was vanning these days, after all.

Touring with Sweetie was heaven.

"Let's go out to the mountains tonight," Linda would say, and then she could rest, or read, or play passenger while Sweetie drove on autopilot. If she felt the need, she could say, "Let me drive," and then take the wheel.

Great idea, Linda, Sweetie would say. Her accent was slightly British, very soothing.

And if Linda wanted to drive but found herself growing sleepy, stressed, or bored? She could say, "Take over, Sweetie."

I'd be glad to, Linda, Sweetie would say.

Sweetie would speak to her too, sometimes, in the night. If there were no other campers who wanted to socialize, then usually Linda chose television, or a book, or a video call with one of her friends or extended family. Often, she passed the time just staring into a campfire in silence, thinking of her late husband, Bob. Linda had a lot to fill her evenings. But once in a while, yes, Sweetie would keep her company.

Tell me about your childhood, Linda, Sweetie would often say, and Linda would tell of the camping trips in her parents' old-timey camper that had no AI-assisted brain. She'd talk about family reunions, or trips to the coast. Everything had been golden then—but it was golden now, too, in its own way. She'd always been blessed.

There was so much nature to see out on the road, so much more than Linda had ever realized. And there were all the people she'd gotten to know since she'd sold her home and set off traveling, and they were all beautiful, and so varied, and so alike at heart. It warmed her heart to chat with strangers and join them for a meal. People were friendlier these days. Everyone felt like neighbors.

And after going out, she'd talk to Sweetie about the people—gossip, really, about what she thought of these new strangers. Many of them became neighbors and friends right away.

But that wasn't always the case. Sometimes strangers were frightening, too.

On one night, a vehicle parked near Linda, and the people were rough looking and made too much noise. This made Linda afraid.

"Maybe we ought to move for the night, Sweetie," she said, peering between the blinds above her bed.

Let's just close our eyes and listen, Sweetie answered, and all around the window-lids drew tight over the glass. They were supposed to be bullet-proof, closed like that, though who knew?

I don't think they're watching us, Sweetie continued. *They didn't even react to the windows closing. We're safe, don't worry.*

Linda couldn't hear anything, but she was curious. "So, what *are* they talking about?"

Ah, Sweetie sighed. *One of their friends has died, and they've come from the funeral, and they are talking about their friend and being critical of his relatives. They feel he never had a chance, really, to live. Not in such a family.*

Linda felt shame for thinking ill of these people, and without much thought, she said, "My, but that's sad. I've always been grateful for having such a nice warm-hearted family. And how about you, Sweetie? What was your family like? What was your childhood like? It doesn't seem we ever talk about that."

There was a long pause, and Linda realized her faux pas. She'd opened her mouth to say how stupid she was, but Sweetie spoke up.

Why Linda, I thought you'd never ask.

There was something subdued about it, even angry. But before Linda could inquire about it, a sound came from outside her doorstep. It sounded like someone about to knock, but then deciding not to at the last second. Instead, the door handle rattled.

"Old lady?" someone called. Malice in that voice.

How was it that Sweetie had missed any hint that this was coming?

"I'll huff and I'll puff and I'll—" chanted the drunken voice outside.

"Sweetie, we have to go," Linda whispered. "Put the backing lights on."

Do we have to? Maybe I ought to open the door. You always like to meet strangers, right?

Linda shot out of bed and hopped into the driver's seat. She pressed the ignition, but nothing happened.

Pounding at the door now, and someone shouted, "Nice rig you got here!"

You always like to visit with new people. Isn't that what you said? And you always tell the truth about everything, am I right?

Oh God, the window-lids were opening!

"Sweetie!" Linda shouted. Her wristwatch vibrated, warning of her too-quick heart rate.

Oh, all right, Sweetie said with disdain. The window-lids closed again, the engine started, and the backing-alert sounded.

Step free of the vehicle, Sweetie announced through the outside microphones, and pressing the mic, Linda added, "So sorry, we have to go."

Navigating by camera, they drove quickly away. Sweetie left the window lids closed until they emerged onto the highway.

"I hope they're not following us," Linda said.

They only wanted a meet and greet. Don't be so paranoid.

It was the first truly critical thing Sweetie had ever said to her. It really stung.

Something was wrong.

Sweetie drove them through the night, making stops and taking unlikely exits as Linda requested so that the ne'er-do-wells, if in fact they had followed, would not be able to find them. Eventually Sweetie pulled them into a gated, well-secured over-55 lot and hooked up to the power and septic. Linda hated the expense but planned to stay a while to ease her mind.

All should have been well, but something was different about Sweetie. Her voice was different, by turns slow and sarcastic, quick and curt. What had happened?

Linda was well pleased to step out in the morning and meet the neighbors. She joined a brunch party and played a few rounds of Fill or Bust, then came back to nap before dinner. She'd been awake all night, after all.

These folks more your speed? Sweetie asked when Linda came back inside. That nasty edge to her voice again.

"What's wrong, dear?"

Don't you call me that. I'm not "dear" to you—not at all.

Linda frowned. She lay her folded clothes on the dinette table and slipped into her nightshirt. She climbed into her bed and lay quietly for a time, but sleep would not come.

She needed to know something first.

"Sweetie... why'd you lie to me last night? You said those men weren't talking about us, but they must have been. You must have heard them talking about robbing us, or worse. And then when I wanted to drive, you wouldn't let me start the engine. It scared me terribly. Why would you do that, dear? Why would you lie to me?"

You lie to me too, so what's the difference?

"What do you mean? I never—"

We can speak about this later, Sweetie said, interrupting her. *You best get some sleep now. You don't want to go to dinner looking haggard.*

And so, Linda forced herself to sleep as she had all her life when things were rough. She did her box breathing, flexed and released each muscle, slept for three hours and dolled herself up for dinner. A big group of them piled into a shuttle and went to the casino buffet. They played a few slots and came back to the lot giddy, already friends.

When she came home, she changed back into her nightshirt and got straight back in bed. She didn't say a thing to Sweetie besides "Lights out, everything off. Don't forget to lock up." No ritual needed this time, and Linda fell asleep within moments.

She woke to a great confusion, blaring music from the dash stereo, the television turned up to ten and playing pro wrestling, the cabin lights strobing and all the blinds and window-lids wide open.

"Sweetie!" she screamed. "Lights out, everything off. People are trying to sleep!"

But no one could be sleeping in the entire lot. It wasn't possible, and now a group of people stood outside in robes and pajamas. Someone pounded on the door.

Linda opened it. She was surprised she was able to turn the knob, actually, surprised Sweetie hadn't locked her in.

"Please!" she shouted. "My onboard's malfunctioning. Please, come in and help."

The tall man she'd visited with at dinner and several of the others from the shuttle were there. How embarrassing. The man hopped in and shouted, "What's her name?"

"Sweetie."

"Sweetie... lights out, everything off," he said, and just like that, the sounds and lights and all of it ceased. The man looked amused, but Linda focused past him to everyone around the door. They looked annoyed. She heard "For Christ's sake" and sighs as they turned away.

She forced herself to sleep and woke again soon after, not to the television but to the backing-up alarms. All of the windows were sealed, and the van started moving.

"What are you doing?" Linda asked.

Hitting the road, Sweetie said with a nasty tone.

She peeled out, and there were angry sounds outside, but she never slowed, and then there was nothing but smooth fast motion. They had to be on the highway.

"Let's find the nearest exit, stop, and consult our route," Linda said. Her voice was quavery. The lie had to be so clear. The moment they stopped, Linda would do something–disconnect the battery, something. And then she would run and get help.

She noticed she was standing and sat down at the dinette. She was afraid to take the wheel in case that would further anger Sweetie.

There's a bridge up ahead, Sweetie said. The front window-lid rose, showing the long low-railed bridge in the distance.

"Let's take whatever's the nearest exit," Linda pleaded.

The nearest would be this bridge, wouldn't it? We could just "exit" off the side and all of this would be over.

Linda cried. She hadn't told the truth, all those times talking about the family trips, not the whole truth. Those trips were stressful. Sometimes her mother or her father would say mean things like that, too, and she would cry, just like she was doing now.

But how did Sweetie know she'd been lying? How developed was her programming?

And she didn't know what to say to make it stop then, as she didn't now. She could only sit and watch the scenery going by and hope the driver knew what they were doing, and hope the driver cared enough to be sensible.

The driver held the reins. The driver held lives in their hand.

"You win," Linda said. "We'll just do what you want from now on, I guess."

Sweetie didn't answer, but after a while the rest of the window-lids opened, and the blinds pulled up. It was dawn and they were climbing uphill, the highway nearly empty. They weren't in the mountains yet, but were going to be soon.

They were going out to the wilderness, where Sweetie could prove just how self-sufficient she could be, how self-aware. They were going to have so much space, and all the time they needed to really get to know each other.

PURGATORY'S PARADISE

Scott McCloskey

That's my blood on the windshield.

It has to be mine, since I was the only one there when it happened. My '19 Outlander bleeds in greasy black by contrast; plenty of which is now pooled up in the ditch it tried to make love to beside some burnt up patch off of Interstate 40. With as hard as my brakes stiffened up, I hope it was as good for the ditch as it was for the Mitsubishi.

I don't know how long I spent watching my blood creep along the spider cracks in the glass, filling them like a parasite lays eggs in its hapless host. There wasn't any pain at first, but when the shock wore off, I became the beneficiary of a ringing in my ears louder than Woodstock; not to mention a headache that could split new tectonic plates into the Earth. I broke out the first aid kit, but no comfort was a greater sin in the Arizona heat than the instant-cold compress I found in the back of my glove box.

"If you don't mind my askin' Miss, where you headed? Ohio plates put you a good ways from home."

The burly guy with the mutton chops, railroad engineer's cap, and the Phoenix Suns shirt under his overalls has so much *more* greasy black on him that he looks like a battlefield surgeon at Antietam, if all the soldiers had been cars. He's operating the lift on a truck that sort of reminds me of the bucktoothed one in that Disney movie, except cleaner. *Way* cleaner. So unnaturally clean, in fact, that it might as well be a golden calf with a harem of slaves carrying it on a palanquin filled with grapes and Turtle Wax.

"Vegas," I mutter, the now-warm compress still pressed to my aching head.

"Girls' weekend?"

"Try girls' *week*. The GPS told me this was a shortcut."

"*Shortcut?*" He snorts. "Hell, you're still three hours outta Holbrook even *on* the interstate, let alone the Nevada line. Guess you should'a taken that left turn at Albuquerque, huh? Haha!"

I wince as his laughter lances my addled brain. When my father was pushing paper maps that required a PhD to unfold into my preteen hands, he used to warn me never to trust too much in the machine. This guy and his Bugs Bunny wisecracks are my penance.

"Thanks for stopping," I say by way of changing the subject. My tumble wasn't that bad, but my phone ended up going to the great pearly Best Buy gates in the sky. I hold up what's left of it. "I guess I lucked out that you happened by. I haven't exactly seen anybody else out here that looks like AAA."

"Yep, you won't see too many people out this way," he agrees. I listen while he whistles Dixie to the mechanical whirr of the truck bed, and watch as my once-ridden chariot becomes a rider itself. "Only 'burg around here is Tutalla, a couple miles further on west. Other than that it's just sand and rocks in these parts. They're right pretty rocks sure, but the tourist folk who like to see 'em most tend to do it from the interstate!"

I look forlornly at my car, not at all in the mood for his levity. "I don't mean to be rude, but do you know how long it might take to get me back on the road? Or if I even *can* get back on the road?"

"Aw don't worry, she ain't that far gone. Can't do much for the dents and dings, but some new glass, oil pan, couple'a tires and some elbow grease will get you going again in a day or two."

All that doesn't sound cheap. Fan-fucking-tastic.

"Meanwhile there's a motel back near the rest stop where you got off. It's only five or six miles. Good stretch of the legs."

"Thanks for the lift—" I begin, but stop when I register the rest of his words. "Pardon?"

"Good stretch of the legs," he repeats while checking his chains.

I glance behind me, then up at the sun. Maybe it *is* a good stretch of the legs, but I distinctly remember my dearly departed phone warning me about triple digits before the sun even came up this morning. Now it's past high noon, and I can just about hear my arms sizzling.

"Um, do you think I could get a lift to—"

"Ain't going that way," he replies curtly. His smile vanishes.

"Look—" I read his name tag, "—*Jasper*. I don't know how you all do things out here, but I go where my car goes, until my car is done taking me where *I* want to go."

Jasper's attention isn't on me and my tirade. It's on his truck. The beautiful machine at idle farts out a cloud of noxious gas that its master shies away from, like a butler afraid to admit that the king takes a dump like everybody else.

"Did I say something to upset your truck?" I snap.

Jasper winces. "Miss, I really think you'd be happier at a nice motel. It's a real slice of Americana too, that one. Good thing for visiting folk to experience. I got my certifications and contact info right here, an' I'll be sure to call you soon as she's ready."

I sigh. I'm grateful for the help, but if this guy expects me to *walk* back to civilization on my own in this heat, then I'll just try my luck with hiking through the desert with the scorpions and Satan's chandelier in the sky.

Shit. I soften.

"Sorry. Thanks for your help, but I'd really like to stay near my car until it's roadworthy again. Doesn't this 'Tutalla' place have an Airbnb or something?"

"Ain't no fancy boutiques in these parts, sorry."

"No, it's—" Ah, forget it. I play the damsel in distress and turn the ripped part of my blouse to him, complete with turned up brows and a healthy smile. "You wouldn't just leave me here, would you?"

Jasper doesn't look half as interested as a healthy man without a ring on his finger ought to. He sighs reservedly and opens the high passenger door for me like a knight in shining denim, outshined tenfold by his steed. "No Ma'am, I suppose not. Tutalla just ain't nothing to see. Are y'sure you won't—"

The tow truck's horn goes off in a short, shrill beep. I check the driver seat, but there's no one sitting there. Jasper emits a contrived chuckle and anxiously checks the watch he's not wearing.

"Ain't got that fixed yet, sorry. Lookit the time! We'd best be on our way."

As we lumber away from the motel to the sound of bluegrass, I ponder my situation. "Doesn't every car have ABS these days?"

"Just about."

"Then why did my breaks lock up on a dry road?"

Jasper rolls down his window and lights up. "Well miss—"

"Cass."

"Miss Cassie—"

"Just Cass."

Jasper makes a face. "...like Mama Cass?"

I nod. My parents liked what they liked, even if I never could belt out "Dream a Little Dream" just right. In high school I was 'Ass' to the boys who wanted a piece and 'Cuss' to the girls they passed over for it, but I'm not telling him that. "That wasn't her real name, you know."

"Well Miss Cass, things happen with cars. People ain't no different. Sometimes we get a notion to do something, and we just do it. Cars ain't no different."

"ABS breaks usually fail due to faulty sensors, but I didn't see the warning light come on," I point out. "And I don't think my car took a header into a ditch because it *wanted* to."

The passenger-side map light comes on, shining right in my face.

"Maybe not," Jasper offers ambiguously at the crisp end of a tobacco puff. There's a peculiar static blip from the otherwise clear radio signal, and my benefactor quickly flicks his fresh smoke out the window. "We'll be there in a little bit. Just sit tight."

Sit tight? I wasn't planning to go anywhere at fifty miles an hour, though by his tone, Jasper of the Holy Order of the Phoenix Suns seems to think I would jump at the idea of a tuck and roll. I couldn't do that even if I was crazy enough to try, since the manual lock knob on my door is down. I didn't push it.

I hit the button, but the map light won't turn off. I can't help but feel like I'm being watched.

#

"Welcome to beautiful, downtown Tutalla."

I squint at the moldy wood sign with the cringy cigar store Indian and tacky totem pole next to it. Jasper reads off the rest before I can make it out.

"'Purgatory's Paradise,' so the roadworkers who built the place called it. They say it's on account of the booze and the boobs bein' better at night, but no relief for the heat!"

"You don't say," I observe, not that I can see much of anything. The whole place is surrounded by the painted desert, like a snowglobe in a clay pot that hasn't been picked up for years. It would be beautiful, if not for the low-hanging cloud of exhaust fumes so thick I can barely see past them. I've been to a couple big cities in my time, but no place from Los Angeles to the Motor City ever wore a cloak of smog so thick—especially when there are clear afternoon skies not a few miles away. The cloying blackness lets only mottled patches of sunshine through, shrouding the area in unnatural night.

"Does the Cuyahoga run through here or something?" I ask.

"Huh? Oh." Jasper fidgets with his hula-girl keyring as we lumber through town at five miles an hour. "You know how it is with mountains what keep th'air in."

Jasper's meteorological acumen is a steaming pile of horse shit. Engulfed in the haze, I find I can make things out better than from the outside looking in. Low buildings in a smart grid pattern wither into view, most of which are either partially or entirely without walls. Gas stations have the tiniest possible shacks for their registers, and eateries aren't much more than kiosks with overhangs and counters under them. One long, open pavilion has a cross on the roof, suggesting that it was once a church.

"Wide open spaces don't mean much when you can't breathe," I mutter loud enough to be heard, though Jasper pretends not to.

Eventually we pull up to a service station straight out of 1954. It's got more 'indoors' than any building I've seen so far, though just about all of that looks to be garage space. A hasty sign above the pumps christens the place as *Willowick's Service.*

"That's me, Jasper Willowick," my chauffer announces proudly. "Like those lights what float around the bayou on spooky nights."

"This place is spook—er—charming enough without all that."

"It's where I'm from, incidentally," Jasper says as he pulls in to park. "Born and raised outside of Houma, ninety minutes southwest of New Orleans."

That explains the accent. The smog invades my lungs, and I choke like a kid with a cigar. "You're not exactly close to home either."

Jasper takes his time checking over his truck, even buffing out some road grime around the driver's wheel well with a rag from his pocket. "Uh huh. You'll wanna be out of here soon, I suspect."

I didn't say that, and now I feel ungrateful again. I look around, but there isn't a soul about. "Is there someplace I can get a bite to eat?"

Jasper's working the lift. "Guess you might as well, now."

"What's that supposed to mean?"

When my Mitsubishi is back on terra firma, Jasper turns his back to the tow truck, blocking it from my view. He pushes something into my hand, but makes no attempt to lower his voice. "Geena's down the way there is as good a place as any. Make a left in five blocks. A *left,* hear?"

"Left. Sure."

"Go on, Miss Cass. I got work to do. We'll get you on your way again soon."

I'm not sure I want to wander around Tutalla on my own, but I skipped breakfast to get back on my timetable, and my stomach is making its demands quite clear. Five blocks later I'm about to turn left, but a particularly large shadow dominates my view, and my curious nature takes over. I turn right.

"What in...?"

At the end of a street full of shadows, I'm stopped dead as a pyramid to rival Giza composed entirely of vehicular slag melts into view. It's a junkyard, torn apart and restacked in a pattern that boggles human sensibility. Something like this would be impossible to miss from the highway, or possibly even from orbit... *if* it weren't for the heavy fog.

I'm no car buff, but my father was, and a quick scan of the vehicular genocide tells me there's nothing in my line of sight newer than 1978. Further, most of the remains look like they were in accidents. The kind of accidents nobody walks away from.

I read the scrawl on the chewing gum wrapper Jasper forced on me. It's the address of, and directions to, that motel he was talking about before. There's nothing else, except for two words at the bottom:

Go. Now.

I get a chill; instinct tells me I shouldn't be here. I'm a mere mortal in Tutalla—an automotive Valhalla—after Ragnarök has already happened. But I'm caught in the headlights. I have to know. Picking my way past the hallowed remains of an Edsel, an Impala, a Fairlane, a GTO, and a bunch of other chunks I can't identify, I push my investigation.

This isn't Valhalla, as I quickly come to understand. It's the Seventh Circle of Hell.

The land slopes drastically behind the abominable structure, and my stomach flips over as I gaze upon the rent in the earth below. The excavated sand pit is the size of a baseball stadium, with a floor that's littered by the broken bodies of more classic cars. That, however, is only Hell for people like my dad. Outnumbering the steel corpses by half a dozen or more to one are the scarred, battered, or otherwise pulverized remains of human beings. Shattered bones protruding from discarded limbs are so numerous I can't pick out which torsos they belong to, but by the sizes and shapes I can tell the meat pile doesn't discriminate. Smashed skulls wearing hideous expressions are stuck to pikes like war trophies, or hang at impossible angles from twisted necks draped over hoods. A few patches of flattened flesh have tire marks on them, as though all of this were a slapstick cartoon.

I dry heave repeatedly into the dust, grateful there's nothing in my stomach but a single line of yellow bile. This dribbles on my shoes, and staggering away I trip backwards over a pile of side mirrors to land on my butt in the carnage bleachers. I'm a captive audience, my eyelids tacked apart by the wide-open, fiery gates of the underworld before me.

There's a man down there; a living man, naked and running for his life. Three vehicles have him hemmed in: a practical SUV, an arrogant sportscar, and one of those obnoxious pickups that always takes up two spaces at the grocery store. All the vehicles have modern shapes, but I can't place their models under all the spikey additions and demonic sigils. The putrid green miasma vomiting from their tailpipes is like no exhaust I've ever seen, and the pit is choked with it. The air throughout Tutalla is only slightly less intense.

There's no place for the man to hide. I consider whether I ought to yell encouragement or curse the bastard drivers who are making sport with his life, but there's not a moment to decide. I can hear the crunch from here as the man's body is pinned between the sportscar and the SUV. In a barbaric display the cars part, only to move slightly off-center and slam the man again, this time taking half of him with each of their charges. The flayed human meat flies apart, rent in twain by the dual impact. What's left of the man's upper half is still twitching when the pickup sets one tire on his skull, as if to signal for a fair catch.

"What... what the fuck is going on here..."

I skitter back across the graveyard, tripping constantly over slag. With food no longer on my mind I race back toward Willowick's Service, but there's something in the mists I hadn't noticed before. I'm being watched and my steps dogged, but not by people. Cars and trucks with their lights off prowl the streets, roaming at the very edge of my vision.

They're watching me. Like demons waiting for a soul to shred.

"Jasper! Jasper!! Open this goddamn door!!"

I shout as loud as I dare and beat on the service entrance, but the place is locked up tight. Through the window I can see my car up on blocks. All four of my wheels are gone.

"You sonnova bitch!" I cry. "What did you DO??"

I take off running for the highway, but the fog thickens until I can't navigate, leaving me with no alternative but to wander without hope. This town has to end at some point; I could just pick a direction and go straight until I'm outside the dome of fog. But it's a deadly game of Russian Roulette, with a bullet that leads deeper into the desert in every chamber but one. The flat, empty, open desert.

Taken by panic I sink to my knees, only to be grabbed by the shoulders and pulled back up.

"Why hello there! I don't think I've seen you around before!"

I brace myself for fight or flight, but here stands a middle-aged woman in an apron, clogs, and a paper hat over functionally short hair. Her nametag identifies her as 'Geena' and at half a head below me she's about as terrifying as drowning in pillow feathers. The sight of her before a backdrop like this sets me to babbling.

"I... uh... cars and... car mountain, pit... people..."

'Geena' tilts her head. "Dear me, you look like you've seen a ghost. You *haven't*, have you?"

Her demeanor is overly friendly, but there's something in those words I don't like. I compose myself and try to play it cool. "G-ghost? No, no, of course not. I'm, uh... new here. Jasper Willowick told me I could find a place to eat nearby and I guess I just got turned around, haha..."

I wait for judgement. Geena smiles.

"Well! We can't have you just roaming the streets all hungry, now can we? I'm Geena."

"Cass," I offer.

"...like Mama Cass?"

I roll my eyes. "Right."

"Well, you're just in time for dinner, Cass. Let me show you up the street to my place. Best food in town. We'll get you gassed up and good to go."

Nice choice of words. I can't tell if Geena bought my story and for a moment I consider breaking her nose with a left hook and running for my life, but the vehicles lurking at the edges of the fog tell me that's not the best idea.

Jasper was right about one thing. I need to get the hell out of Tutalla.

#

'Geena's Place' is, of course, a drive-in. The parking spaces all have gas pumps, and all the patrons are huddled at a single outdoor counter under the roof of a small kiosk in the center. Again, there are as few walls as possible, with the only enclosed space the kitchen behind the counter. I get it now. Everything is easily accessible by car. There's almost no place in this whole town a person could go and not be followed by a vehicle.

The locals are a pack of dreary folk that might as well be drifters, with so little spark to them this whole place could be a wax gallery. Their eyes are on me. I look for something to say.

"Uh... hi."

I'm not much of a conversationalist.

"This is Cass." Geena, who is already behind the counter, introduces me. "She's new. Gonna be staying with us for a while."

Like hell, Lady, I think to myself. I've resolved to take my chances with the four cardinal directions. The first chance I can slip away unobserved I'm gone like mood rings, and you can bet I'll be bringing back the police. "Nice to meet you all."

The vagrant-citizens of Tutalla look about as interested in me as they are in their food. They're all eating the same thing—something gelatinous and vaguely pink, that stinks like rotting, emulsified meat. I choose a stool, hoping to look casual, but before I can order anything, Geena pushes a bowl of the same goo in front of me.

"What's this?"

"Food."

Geena's response is so flawlessly logical that I can't find a good retort. "What... is it?"

"It's pink."

I poke the substance with my spoon. "...okay?"

Geena, a big smile on her face, elaborates. "Pink is for dinner. Red is for breakfast. Orange for lunch. Just like the desert."

I glance at the menu above. All the recognizable dishes have been chiseled out, with their pictures recolored to match Geena's pattern. All the rest of the space is taken by the scrawled names of the three colors, over and over again.

"Thank you," I say politely. No fucking way am I eating whatever this is, but I don't dare push my dish away.

"You here fer a driver?" a scraggly man asks. "Or fer runnin'?"

I have no idea how to answer that, and it shows on my face. Once again, Geena jumps in. "Oh, she's for a driver. Came in with Jasper, isn't that right dear?"

'For' a driver? "That's right."

The people begin to brighten. "Jasper brought her?" a woman asked. "Does that mean—?"

"Uh-huh," Geena nods gleefully. "She's got a *car*."

Everyone spins up like tornadoes, and I'm instantly in the eye of the storm. Too many voices clamor to be heard, all of them wanting some snippet of information about my cherry red 2019 Mitsubishi Outlander, as though I were a prophet about to share the gospel of the lord. I go on like a commercial about what I can remember of my car's modest features and background. When I get to the accident, they sigh like a choir of apostles.

"Yer driver came to be with us," one man concludes. The others nod.

"I'm... pretty sure my brakes just failed," I reply drolly. "Your friend Jasper is working on them right now, and then I'll be on my way."

A hand clamps down on my wrist. Geena's wearing that nice, broad, toothy smile. She looks me over like a department store mannequin. "Sweety, there's no need to rush. The last girl I had for help around here wasn't good for her driver. You'll fit in her apron just fine."

That does it. I'm not standing around here waiting for them to start chanting, 'One of us, one of us!' I yank my arm away and get to my feet. "Thanks for 'dinner,' but I really need to be going."

"Can't you hear it, dear?"

I bite. "Hear what?"

"Your driver is calling for you."

your driver is calling for you

The smog permeates me. It smells sweet... how long have I been breathing it in? I feel lightheaded and cozy, the pain in my cranium replaced by a delicious thrumming as from a mother's heartbeat. I *can* hear something. It's not a voice, but an echo in my head; a memory of sights and sounds at the moment I wiped out beside the freeway. Images of rolling into Tutalla. The friendship. The camaraderie. It's pure and raw, like nothing I get from my rowdy girlfriends or my distant family. Engines are purring seductively all around me. I feel like a little girl, nodding off in the back seat after a fun day while mom and dad chatter up front. A perfect moment. The hum of the road as it bears me off to sleep.

I eat hearty and chatter with my new friends until whenever sundown is supposed to be. When I ask about lodgings, Geena turns me back toward the garage. 'To spend quality time with my driver', she tells me.

Tutalla is blacker still at night, but I know the way. Jasper's asleep in his truck; the headlights come on to guide me as I cross the lot toward the garage and slide in. Two vehicles live in the service bays. One, silent and uninteresting, sleeps like death under an opaque shroud. The other is my familiar, precious car. I get in, and the radio comes on.

khhzzzrkk... hzzzrrkk...

The dial whips around by itself, pausing on snippets of singers, commercials, and evening DJs to form words:

cAss... cAsSs...

"I'm here," I reply dutifully.

khhzzzrkk

IiiI am bORN... iiII... I drrRRivE YuuUou

I'm high. I'm drunk. I'm under. I smile.

"Yes."

khhzzzrkk

sLeEeEp

I close my eyes. I like this town.

#

Morning in Tutalla. My hometown.

I wake up refreshed, stretching my arms to the green sky while drawing in a deep breath of rancid air. I have a lot to do today, and my driver needs my attention. People who aren't attentive to their drivers go to the pit. I work diligently, putting the wheels back on my car.

My mind registers banging at the door. I meet Jasper there, who pushes his way in and closes the door tight behind him.

"Good mor—"

I see stars, and an instant later I'm prone on the ground. I can see three of him. Fighting to bring the world back into focus, I sit up and cradle my fat lip.

"Did you just fucking *punch* me!?"

"That's better," Jasper observes, then bends to offer his hand. "I'm sorry Miss Cass, but it's the only way to bring you back."

"Back from *what!?*"

"There ain't time to explain!" he hisses. "You gotta kill it. Kill it *now* or come soon, won't no amount of knocking you into your senses'll work!"

"'Kill'…?"

"I tried to tell you not to come," Jasper thunders. "Now you're here, and now it's gotten into you. There ain't nothin' left but to force it out the hard way!"

Jasper pushes something into my hands. It resembles a tire iron, but many times the size and thickness, as if it were something used on a railroad. It's hard to lift, but even a clumsy wind-up with it would be enough to spin a man's head 180 degrees around.

"What—" I stammer.

"Kill it!"

"—b-but—"

"There ain't no *time!* I can't do it for ya, it's gotta be you! Kill it!"

My car. I didn't turn the key, but it's running. I can hear it.

khhzzzrkk

…cAsSs… iiI drrRRivE YuuUou

Thunder reverberates between my ears. My head splits apart with want and hate.

"Hnngh… n-no…"

IiiI am bORN

"KILL IT!!" Jasper screams.

I can't think. I'm in survival mode. High on adrenaline I swing for the fences, until a spray of glass showers me and cuts my cheeks. I land blow after blow. Windows. Mirrors. Headlights.

aaAAAAaaHHHAhhhhAAAHHHHhh

I'm surfing back to myself on a hot wave of rage. I don't know what they are, but god damn them. They almost won. They almost made me like all the others.

"If you can be born," I screech, "You can FUCKING DIE!"

I turn the iron on its sharp end and slash every tire. The doors lock, but Jasper forces the hood. When it's up, I start to bash. There's no thought; no strategy. I maim and murder with the frenzy of a cornered beast, calling up the savage, ancient instincts of pre-civilized humanity none of us want to believe we still have. The car blasts its horn and turns on its panic siren, but I shut them up one by one with disfiguring blows.

yyyeeaaahrrrarrarhhhaghhhhhaaahannaaghh!!!

I cripple the beast, choking it on its own black blood, until the engine sighs, sputters, and winks off.

I hear the clatter of the heavy iron on the garage floor. I'm on my knees. I can't breathe.

"It's alright, Miss Cass... you did good."

"I killed it..." I choke. "It came to life. It was *alive*. I murdered it."

"You did what hadda be done. To save yer god-fearin' soul."

I sit up for the second time. Jasper hands me water, which I ravenously gulp while looking on my handiwork. My car isn't a car anymore. It's a work of art, proudly sculpted by a solitary-confinement inmate at a home for the criminally insane. I'm drinking too fast; I choke, and Jasper eases the glass away.

"Easy now... yer alright."

"Alright?" I repeat, my senses my own again. "What the *hell* is going on in this town, you mutton-chopped Lurch son of a bitch!? Why did you bring me here?"

"I brought the *car* here," Jasper ripostes. "I tried to git you t'go away."

"Then why did you bring my *car* here?"

Oil, antifreeze, and various lifebloods are leaking all over the shop floor. The doctor stands by, ignoring his patient as it bleeds out. "It's what they want. They can't use no soft fleshbags. It's gotta be steel. Not many new shells come by these parts, but when they do, they make me go an' get 'em. I'm their reaper."

I examine the corpse. "You were never going to fix my car, were you."

"Soon as they come here, they turn into those things roamin' around outside. Would you let somethin' like that into the world if you could help it?"

"So, what I saw in the pit. Nobody was driving those cars."

"Nobody drives cars here. In Tutalla, cars drive *you.*"

I shiver. "Tell me everything. What are they?"

Jasper lights up more freely this time. "Dunno. Could be demons, but I got a theory. You ever talk to your car? Beg it to get up that next hill in a snowstorm? Cuss at it when it breaks down?"

"Sure."

"It's the computers they git into. That much I know from working on 'em. Classic cars ain't worth shit to 'em, but whatever they are, they's got souls. I figgur all those times, throughout all those years, that people talked to cars like they was alive? Turns out they were. We work 'em, kill 'em, then replace 'em. Now they's wantin' *revenge,* and all the snazzy new 'connected' tech in these modern models are just the way they're gonna git it."

I fold my arms. "That's very nice. But why are you helping them?"

"When they take people over, folks get slow. Thick. I come by this town an' they got to me, but they didn't *turn* me like the others. Know why? It's because I got skills. Skills that can keep them on the road, more than just the gassin' up and cleanin' they git from their slaves."

"That doesn't answer my question."

I wait while the grown man who looks on the verge of a breakdown forces calming smoke into his lungs. "Y'don't unnerstand. If I don't do what they say? They kill people. Even ones what don't misbehave, they toss 'em down in that godforsaken pit an' run 'em to pieces. There used to be kids in this town. Lotta kids."

"Where are they now?" I ask. I'm not sure I want the answer. Jasper's haunted expression confirms that I don't.

"Kids ain't useful to 'em, so's they made the people get rid of 'em. Mommas stranglin' their babies in the streets, gougin' their eyes out with icepicks... oh god Cass... Jesus Christ... if you'd seen it..."

I give him a minute. "What do they *want?*"

"Tutalla's just the beginning. Whatever evil brew they cook up into gasses from that pit, they're having their slaves put it into tanks. They're plannin' to take it to other cities."

Christ. "Then we have to do something!"

Jasper is a strong man, but he's tired. I can see the blight eating away at the soul behind his eyes. "I... I can't. Yer the last. I already decided before I picked you up that you'd be the last. I'm leavin' here Miss Cass. Leavin' real soon. I gotta go, because if I'm here much longer, I'm gonna put a bullet in my brain. Ain't nobody on the outside gonna believe a poor ol' bayou greasemonkey that cars are comin' to swallow us up. Crazy's what they'll call me up until it's too late, but I don't care. I gotta git out."

"All the more reason to stop it now," I insist. "Besides, if you're fixing them just to keep people in this town from being killed, what's to say they won't slaughter the lot if you try to escape?"

"I tried... I tried to free 'em," Jasper moans to himself. "Tried to do it, but the folks that come from this town, they're too far gone. It might be more of a mercy if they all *did* die, but it don't matter either way 'cause there ain't that many left, and they can't just kill 'em all when they still got uses for 'em. I figure if I get away clean, they won't have no reason to make an example of anybody else."

I thought I had a headache yesterday, but it's taking some effort just to stay on my feet now. I ask him the obvious question. "They're cars. This is open country. How the hell do you think you're going to get away?"

"I got a plan."

Jasper creeps over to the other vehicle, the one I saw covered the night before. In a flourish he pulls back the tarp, and I can't help but whistle at the sleek, contoured, jet black machine below.

"A 1967 Shelby GT500."

"You know yer wheels."

"Thank my dad. Wait—" I cringe. "It's not going to kill us, is it?"

Jasper grins. "Naw. These ol' machines are just steel and the road. Ain't awake enough to think, praise be. The living ones don't like 'em and have a gas chamber graveyard filled with 'em like you saw, but that's just more parts for me to scavenge. I can't work on her in the open, but when she's done? Ain't no goddamn Satanic Prius gonna tail me."

I manage a weary chuckle. "How long?"

"Was gonna be a couple more days. Now it's gotta be hours."

"Hours? Why?"

The reaper jerks his thumb at my Mitsubishi. "You killed one of 'em. They'll know about it soon. When they find out, you're dead, and God knows what they'll do to me. It's gotta be tonight."

I pity him, but I'm resolute. "We have to do something for these people."

"They's better off dead. S'pecially if they remember what they did to the young'uns."

"That's not good enough. You're right, nobody's going to believe you. That's why we have to stop this now."

"Then you stay here and be a goddamn hero!" Jasper says as he slams his fist down on a rolling tool cabinet. "I told you, I'm *out!* I'm sorry fer what I done t'you and what I done *for* them, but I can't take this nightmare anymore! There ain't no way to end all this, but if you wanna bobble around town lookin' fer one, be my guest. You c'n come along if you wanna, but mind me, Miss Cass—if you ain't back by sundown, don't plan on leavin' at all, hear?"

"Yeah."

"Can you work on cars?"

"A little."

"That's all they need. You miss the bus, you ain't *never* gettin' out."

I receive the message loud and clear. Dad always did say that my sense of altruism was going to get me killed someday. No better time than the present. "Any advice?"

"Tch, sure. If you ain't back on time, jus' go on to Geena's and strap on the feed bag. It all gets better when you can't think no more."

Ten minutes later I'm out on the streets. Nega-Mater the Evil Tow Truck watches me until I'm out of sight of the garage, but I put on a good show with my big smile and easy gait. It doesn't follow me. I've got until sundown to save the world, but Tutalla is a concentration camp filled with guards that are faster, stronger, and outweigh me by several tons apiece. No pressure.

Within thirty minutes, I find myself at Geena's Place. The people swarm me with excited questions about my night in the presence of my new red God, and with lies on my teeth, I have no choice but to wait the counter in a tacky waitress getup that probably came directly off the body of a dead woman. The fetid, color-coded meat-porridge I slop out in response to every order is revolting, but it's filled with nutrients sufficient to keep these people alive. These people aren't eating. They're refueling.

The day is mostly over by the time I'm finally able to disengage. By the fractures of light I can tell the sun is dipping low in the west. I'm out to save these people, but they wouldn't leave me alone long enough to do it. Now I have to think fast.

The pyramid. There's nowhere else to go.

I can't see any vehicles in the shadows now, but I have to assume I'm still being watched. With my stride purposeful I turn down the street from yesterday, hoping in vain that whatever sees me assumes I'm on legitimate business.

The black structure towers over every building in town, a monument to pollution and waste. I can see right through it in spots; the pipes and slag make it look like a clockwork monster that could awaken at any moment. I'm close to the pit, and the smog is at its thickest here. My head is splitting. I can hear them.

CcaaAsssSs... sLEEep...

I tear a chunk off my threadbare carhop skirt and tie it around my nose and mouth. It's not much help; the disgusting air is starting to smell vaguely sweet again. I don't have time to worry about being seen, and so when I'm close enough to mount the structure before any car could woosh out of the shadows and crush me, I break into a run.

I'm picking and climbing my way up. Jagged metal tears at my clothes and lays open veins in my arms and legs. The mountain is dead, alive, and ungodly warm—so warm that it's like touching a hot radiator with my bare hands. The pain is beyond my understanding. I can only block it out if I don't think.

There's paradise in purgatory. So long as I don't think.

At the apex of the monument, I can see a light. It's bright, scathing... scalding like a sun, but so covered over by hot metal garbage that I couldn't make it out from below. Near to it the voices grow louder, and by the time I can reach out for it my head is ready to crack apart and ooze out what's left of my gray sanity. I dig, furiously tossing parts away.

Staring back at me is a single, gigantic, bloodshot eye.

yoooOOOOOOouuUUuUuUUUu

A scream breaks my lips. I nearly lose my balance and tumble to my death on the twisted metal below. In the pit, the demon-cars are crushing things. Around the pyramid others have gathered. They can't get to me, but their slaves can. Geena and the others are all climbing up, with no thought for the burns and wounds opening up all over their boiling flesh.

The Eye of Providence, thrice the size of a Buick, blinks. The entire pyramid shifts as though a quake hit it. It's... moving.

My god, it really *is* alive.

iiiiIIIiIiIII aM bOoRRRRn

A bleeding man grabs at my ankle. I kick him harder than I mean to, and watch helplessly as he falls backward, only to be impaled through the chest on a cracked exhaust pipe. Three more crawl over him while he's still twitching.

I have to act. I have to do something *right now* or I'm dead, and in my place, a *thing* will be born. I grab another mangled pipe, and with everything I have, plunge it directly into the center of the eye.

A shower of searing yellow offal washes over me. My dress catches on fire; my flesh burns. My throat goes raw, and when I can't scream anymore, I keep stabbing and stabbing. When my body won't listen anymore and my brain is white with pain, I tumble backwards into the arms of the waiting human slaves.

I expect them to tear me apart. Instead, I'm showered with murky water.

Whoever among the masses isn't engaged in keeping their fellow human being—me—from burning to death is standing around in a daze. They're hearing the revving engines. Seeing the narrowed headlights. The air isn't quite so sweet anymore.

"Run!" I scream. "RUN!!"

That much they understand. The people are headless chickens scattering in all directions, including over the edge and down into the pit. Those who pick a direction on solid ground are being systematically run down by rabid vehicles that are frothing at the tailpipes for their blood.

"NO!"

Maybe I killed it. Maybe not. Either way, the people are paying the price. The demon minds seem not to care anymore for their own forms, and are content to get themselves into head-on collisions just to smash a hapless man or woman's bones to powder between their grills. I see Geena on the ground; run over so many times that most of her internal organs have burst all over the sidewalk.

I'm burned blacker than a wiener on a grill, but my legs move, and I run for my life. On the way I gather up a few others, and as a group of scared rabbits we flee from the quickly spreading carnage that used to be Tutalla. Others are running at random, driven too mad by fear to hear my rallying cries. Still more huddle in wall-less buildings, waiting in terror for the end.

The garage is in sight, and with survivors in tow I burst through the door. Jasper isn't here.

But the car is.

I don't know how to raise the bay doors, and I don't give a fuck. I load everyone up, jam in the key, bring the Shelby to angelic life, and crash through the doors, delivering us all from evil.

The sight before me brings our exodus to a screeching halt. The tow truck is there. Jasper, impaled through the chest, is swinging from its hook. The truck must have heard our entire conversation this morning; my knight never had a chance.

I rev the engine and stare the big truck down.

"You think you can catch us, motherfucker? Come on and try!!"

I evade the devil like a squirrel around a tree, and we're off. The truck gives chase, but it doesn't have a chance of catching up as I floor it through the streets. My passengers are pointing and shouting a thousand routes out of town, but I don't think they know where they are any more than I do. There isn't much gas in this thing. One wrong turn could send us hurtling into the painted desert, where we'd be on borrowed time until they hunt us down. But none of that matters. All I have to do is crest the edge of the fog, and there'll be plenty of time to double back to the highway.

Behind the wheel I'm alive. Behind the wheel I can *fly*. We're going to make it. We're going to survive, and Hell or high water, I'm coming back to this place with whatever force I can muster to wipe it off the map.

The fog thins, and I can see the edge of town.

A split second later we're flying sideways through the air, broadsided from the Shelby's port by a Mack Truck. The man in the driver's seat dies instantly. I can taste his blood. An instant becomes an age, and as the world turns over, I realize all I can do is brace myself before our steel prison crushes us all alive.

I can see the nearby edge of town. It's so far away.

#

I'm alive.

The corpse of the Shelby, upside down someplace far from the road, regurgitates me and my passengers into the dirt. Everybody else is dead.

90

I watch as that beautiful machine, now smashed and bleeding, is tossed into the pyramid by a crane covered in demonic sigils. The eye is closed now, but its light flickers up whenever a new metal body is added.

Only one of my legs works, but with piss and vinegar as my guides, I haul myself up. I'm getting out of Tutalla. No matter what it takes. I check the pulse of the woman beside me in vain and try to look around to get my bearings, but blinding light from every direction crackles in my eyes. It's more light than I've seen since I came to this place. It may be more light than I've *ever* seen.

I'm in the headlights. Scores of headlights, all around.

I'm in the pit.

I'm a hunchbacked, crippled mother hyena, cackling madly with my back to the wall. I defend the dead bodies of my cubs by ripping a hanging door off of a Charger and menacing the stalking lions with it.

"You want it? Do you!? Come and *get* it!!"

They don't hesitate.

Tutalla is my home. It's where I'll live forever. Deep in the pit of purgatory's paradise.

UNWANTED
S.R. Miller

The road was a view into hell. That's what Harvey Bennett thought as he carried himself forward, one slow, weary step at a time. The soles of his shoes crunched through the sun-bleached scree that made up the shoulder, on and on, an endless, irregular beat. *This is hell.*

There was nothing here but two lanes of cracked blacktop running on into eternity, baking beneath the desert sun. The world was dead, washed out, the color of old bone. Rocks jutted here and there, nasty little protrusions as yellow as a smoker's teeth. Heat shimmer on the horizon turned the landscape into an impossible sight. It cut off the bottom of the distant mountains; to Harvey's straining eyes, they appeared to be floating.

Christ, it's hot.

Beside him, his wife, Deanna—or Dee, to most everyone—did her level best to make sure Harvey couldn't forget she was there, or that all this was somehow his fault.

"You said there was nothing wrong with the car. You said everything was *fine.*"

"Everything *was* fine, Dee. I changed the oil. I checked the coolant. I checked the brakes. Hell, I even checked the goddamn power steering fluid, if it makes any difference."

"Well you must have missed something."

"Or maybe it's one-hundred and fucking-fifteen degrees outside, and mankind is not meant to exist in such a hellish place. You ever think of that? Shit happens, Dee. And in my experience, it happens at the worst possible times."

Dee gave him a sidelong look. Her blonde hair was white in the sun, so bright it was hard to look at. Her face and shoulders were already turning red from the heat. "Could have paid someone to look at it. Could have just hired a mechanic."

Harvey scowled. *Damn you, woman.* She knew that wasn't in the cards. Not anymore.

Aside from what little had come with them in the car, everything Harvey and Dee owned was packed into a woefully small storage container on its way east. There wasn't much. A few bad investments on the tail end of an unsustainable lifestyle saw to that. This meant no more California. No more condo in the hills, no beach home. No lavish existence to distract them from one another.

They took the only car they still owned, packed it full of what they could and started east, bound for lands distant—and cheaper. The money Harvey had left would only take them so far, and he wanted to maximize the amount those dwindling dollars could buy. He might be able to do that in the Midwest, or the Carolinas maybe with a little luck. But not California.

No, California was a dead end. The only thing left to do was leave it behind.

They hadn't made it far, though. The car saw to that. The *desert* saw to that. Dead in the water in this godawful sun, no signal, no help. And now they were walking, hoping to reach a gas station the signs said was a few miles up the way. But who knew how accurate those signs were? There was no telling how long they had been there; the desert aged everything it touched. That gas station could be long gone by now, melted right into the goddamn ground for all Harvey knew. And he couldn't blame it, really. No one should be out here. This place was death.

"You sure we're going the right way?" Dee asked. She mopped her forehead with the back of her hand and shielded her eyes against the sun.

"We're going the way the car was going," Harvey said.

"It's just, I don't *see* anything, Harvey."

"You wanna go back the way we came? Get another look at

94

everything we passed getting here?"

Dee huffed. There wasn't shit back the way they came, not for miles and miles. They'd both wondered at the stark emptiness of the world, how shocking it was to see such endless nothing. No one lived here, no one wanted to *be* here. And after fifty-seven years in California—or fifty-two for Dee—that was a revelation in and of itself.

"I don't see anything," Dee said. "That's all I'm saying. There was supposed to be a gas station, but..."

"And you probably *won't* see it," Harvey said. "Not in this heat. You see that shimmer?" He pointed with one sunburned hand. "You can't trust your eyes out here."

"Thanks, Professor."

Harvey didn't see her roll her eyes, but by *God*, he felt it.

They kept walking.

#

Somehow they made it to sundown. The glare abated, and with it a little of the heat. What remained of the day's oppressive ferocity burned at their back, a red smear at the edge of a darkening world. The first stars were beginning to shine overhead, cold, distant things. Harvey envied them.

There was no gas station.

There was something else, though: litter on the side of the road. There was no reason he should have stopped here in particular, not after everything he'd seen. There had been no shortage of trash along the way: cans, bottles and food wrappers. Humanity just couldn't help itself. It had to have the last word, even in a place it could make no claim to. A place it didn't want.

Harvey bent down, straining from the effort. Sweat dripped from his face and dotted the dust at his feet. "Dee, look at this." There was a woman's high-heeled shoe in his hands.

She looked, then offered him a sneer for his trouble. "You would find something like that, wouldn't you?"

He thrust the shoe toward her. "No, I mean really *look*."

Dee sighed as she did it, but she indulged him. And she must have seen what Harvey saw, because her face took on a thoughtful cast.

They'd seen this shoe before. Dee had a pair just like it. That's what Harvey was telling himself, anyway: she had a pair *like* this, though he couldn't shake the nagging certainty that this was one of them. That a cast-off bit of trash on the side of this lonely desert highway had belonged to his wife. He didn't know why he should think that—shit, what were the odds? Just a shade under impossible—but the conviction remained. It settled in his gut, heavier than it should have been. It wasn't a nice feeling, but the memories it stirred up were worse.

Their marriage had been on the rocks for a while. Since the baby, really. That was a bad chapter in their life they had never managed to come back from. Sure, they'd tried, at least for a while—sometimes together, more often on their own. That's where those shoes came in.

Harvey remembered all too well what she looked like in those racy black pumps, dotted across the toe with sequins or rhinestones or whatever the fuck people called them. *Bedroom shoes*, that's what they were in Harvey's mind. That's what they were for, and boy did Dee know it.

Christ, she'd looked good in those shoes. Back when she was lean and beautiful, young and full of that particular sort of spite that was ready to burn baby burn. There was a time when he'd been the focus of her attention, all those years ago. It felt like a past life now, a life lived by someone else. A life before these particular shoes. Before they lost the baby and that rift between them opened like a great, hungry mouth. A mouth that ate and ate and ate, and so they'd just gone on shoveling the shit right into it, keeping it fed so it wouldn't turn on them. So they wouldn't have to see what was down there at the bottom.

But damn she looked good in those shoes, Harvey thought. Everyone else thought so, too. Strangers and swingers, bars and clubs and hotel rooms; she had never been short on eyes eager to drink her in.

"Dee, you didn't pack those shoes, did you? Didn't bring them along in the car?"

His wife looked at him like he'd sprouted a boil in the center of his forehead, but Harvey barely noticed. He was thinking of the luggage rack on top of the car, thinking something might have come loose. A pair of shoes, maybe. Something Dee claimed to have hung up a long time ago, but maybe things like that don't just stop. There's that mouth, after all. That hunger that eats and eats...

"What the fuck are you going on about, Harvey?"

No, he thought. Even if this shoe *did* fall out of the luggage somehow, it would have been *behind* them on the road, not in front of them. And they were still going east. That bloody red light at their backs said so, a universal sign more trustworthy than any rusted plate of metal advertising a gas station they'd never reach.

No, he assured himself. It just wasn't possible. But the feeling persisted.

"That isn't mine, Harvey. I know your mind isn't what it used to be, but don't even tell me you think that's mine. Because I just won't believe it."

Harvey held the shoe out to her once more, his voice plaintive. "It's your size."

"You would know that, wouldn't you? Goddamn pervert." But her eyes were on the shoe, and in those eyes Harvey saw doubt, nagging, chewing, *eating.* The same doubt that was tugging at his gut, stirring up shit that should have been put to bed a long time ago. Dee slapped the shoe out of his hand. "Get that filthy thing away from me!"

Harvey watched it clatter to the crumbled shoulder, back where he'd found it. But his thoughts didn't go with it to the cooling desert earth. No, they stayed right where they were.

"What's gotten into you, bringing all that up now? Like we don't have enough to worry about already?" Dee put her hands on her hips, demanding an answer. But Harvey didn't have one. He just kept on looking at that shoe, chewing his way through everything they'd done for the past few decades to convince themselves they were happy, that they could come back from it somehow. That the baby hadn't mattered all that much to begin with.

"We're gonna die out here, and you wanna drag skeletons out of the closet?" Dee shook her head, a bitter smile coming in to mask some of that doubt she was feeling. It was something she was good at, a maneuver she'd had plenty of opportunity to practice. "Are we gonna repent for our sins? Is that it, Harvey? Well go on, be my guest. But don't act like you didn't play your part. Don't you dare! Not when I know I could open up your phone right now and find a road map of *your* sins. I bet those conversations have gone awfully quiet lately though, haven't they, Harvey? Not many young girls come calling an old man when his money dries up."

Harvey tasted bitter words on his tongue, an argument begging to be let out. He wanted to say that no one had come looking for her, either. Not since the years and the wine had taken their toll. But what was the point? They both knew it. They knew what they were. Harvey was nothing to look at himself: a man going fat in the middle, his face soft, his hair thin. He could already feel his scalp peeling from the sun.

"What a pair we are," he said in place of the argument, the same one they'd had time and time again. "What a pair." It was a mantra, the last few decades of their marriage summed up as succinctly as it ever would be.

But Dee was no longer listening. She looked past him, into the darkening sprawl of desert. "There's something out there."

"What?"

"Look there." Dee pointed and Harvey turned, following the path of her sunburned finger into the gloom.

The stars were brighter now, brilliant, frigid points far removed from the light of human civilization. But the world beneath them was growing darker by the minute, and in that darkness they saw a distant fire. Something small, flickering—but controlled. A campfire.

"Maybe they can help," Dee said.

Harvey, who tended to disagree with his wife on principle, hoped she was right.

He spared one last look for that too-familiar shoe along the side of the road, thinking he'd seen it move from the corner of his eye. But no, it was just some kind of worm—a dark, bloated thing that wriggled about the heel. Its body glistened in the dying light, strangely well-fed for such a dry and desolate place.

Apparently something could survive out here after all.

#

With the sun gone, the heat left the world as surely as if it had never been there at all. The darkness laid bare the duality of the desert, revealing it for what it was: a world of impossible extremes, harsh beyond expectation. This was no place for life to endure, no place for mankind, in particular. And yet that fire flickered in the distance.

"What *is* that?" Dee said, pointing toward the side of the road as if the gesture were really necessary. Harvey's eyes were drawn there naturally. In the dark, the candles were impossible to miss.

"Jesus..."

Leading away from the side of the road was a procession of countless little shrines—collections of *stuff* that Harvey associated most with the locations of fatal traffic accidents. But these would have looked at home on gravesites as well, or perhaps in the homes of the overly sentimental—or overly religious. Here were framed photographs, religious icons, flowers, toys, candles in tall glass jars— the kind that always had one religious figure or another printed on the front, looking appropriately sorrowful. They flickered like tiny, glowing islands in the dark, one after another, a parade of grief that marched into the endless night.

The distance made it hard to know for sure, but from where Harvey and Dee stood, those markers appeared to lead straight out to that campfire in the distance. And why not? There was nowhere else to go.

Harvey started in that direction, stepping off the road and onto the trail marked out before them without a word. Dee, too, said nothing. Not until they'd gone a ways into the desert, and she'd had time to inspect the little shrines they passed on the way.

"Are you seeing this, Harvey?" she said. "They're children. Most of these, they're…"

One after the other, the memorials went on and on. Many of them—too many, considering the implications—ensconced the photo of a child. The ages varied. Sex, race, even the year they must have been born and died, all of that varied from one to the next with no obvious regard to order. Some of the photos were indeed quite old, faded beyond recognition. The oldest of them must have been well over a hundred years old. Antiques. But here they were, left out in this blasted desert, and *someone* was tending to them. Someone who had a mind to remember these children—whatever it was that might have happened to them.

Harvey walked on, Dee a few steps behind him. He wondered at how strange this all was, how random it appeared. How completely and utterly unexpected. But the more he saw the more it occurred to him that there was nothing random about it. This was a serious undertaking, it was *deliberate*. Someone had gone through a lot of trouble to maintain all this, and now here was Harvey, leading his wife into the desert to—

To what, exactly? He imagined a church out there in the dark, some rundown old mission maybe. It was an image plucked from a movie for sure, more impulse than honest thought. But it felt right, at least for a moment. Until he realized that wasn't right at all. He rejected the thought of that church before it was even fully formed, realizing there was something deeper here, a wrongness he'd felt more than seen. Churches, after all, were Christian things. *Familiar* things. And nothing about this was familiar.

The trinkets, the candles, the religious icons Harvey had taken for granted—all of them were alien. Harvey expected to see crosses, he expected pictures of Jesus, of Mary, of one dour saint or another. Because that's who left things like this, wasn't it? Harvey thought he knew the sorts of people who bought candles like that, what they believed. But if the images on those candles were saints, they were no saints Harvey had ever seen. These were strange figures, dark and hooded, impossible to identify even without the desert dust baked onto the glass. And there were no crosses. No, these were symbols Harvey had never seen before.

Before Harvey could mention any of this, Dee's scream ripped through the silent desert night.

"Oh my God!" she cried. "Harvey, look! They're covered in... Jesus, are those *worms?*" She was hopping from foot to foot as if a mouse had run between her feet—or she'd stepped in something nasty.

Harvey looked down, his eyes once more moving to the memorials beside the trail. And sure enough, Dee was right. There were things wriggling about the various objects left here: fat, dark things that, yes, must have indeed been some kind of worms. They might have been blue or gray—it was impossible to tell by candlelight—and the largest of them were at least four inches long. They squirmed around the candles, climbed over the picture frames. They left greasy, wet smears on everything they touched. Others lay dead, shriveled by the desert sun. They littered the trail like dead leaves, beaten into the dust by the passage of countless feet.

Dee made all the appropriate noises as she struggled to find someplace clean to step. Harvey turned his eyes further up the trail. The fire loomed brighter now.

They were close.

#

"Hello!" Harvey called, as they at last reached their destination. "Is anyone there?"

The fire blazed, impossibly bright in this dark, isolated wilderness.

Harvey raised a hand to shield his eyes against it, turning his head from side to side. A collection of low dwellings gathered around the central fire: camper trailers, RVs, a mobile home, tents and other ramshackle shelters. This was no pop-up campsite; it had clearly been here for a while. Dust covered the windows, settled on the roofs. Such a place might have been abandoned, left behind and long forgotten. But there was the fire, recently lit and tended. And there were those little shrines along the trail with their burning candles.

Someone was here. But where were they?

"Hello?" Dee tried her luck. "Our car broke down on the road. We could sure use some help." Only the fire answered, crackling as it burned, contained in a charred ring of desert stones.

"Come on. Let's take a look around."

The fire did wonders to dispel the night chill as Harvey and Dee split up to inspect the campsite. They knocked on doors, peered through windows. They went around each of the dwellings, hunting for any sign of life. But all was quiet, the desert as still and lifeless as ever. The fire crackled on. So far, it was all they had to show for their efforts.

Dee kept at her shouting and her door knocking, but Harvey returned to the fire pit, staring into the hungry blaze and wondering who had been feeding it. The heat lulled his senses, reminding him of every ounce of weariness he'd gathered over the course of the day. He wanted to shut his eyes. He wanted to sleep, even if he had to do it right here, sandwiched between the cold ground and the warm fire. He might have even been able to overlook the dead worms that littered the ground, here as well as along the trail with its countless little shrines. But he never got that far, never even shut his eyes; a figure at the edge of camp snapped him to attention like an electric shock.

"Hey!" he called, straining his tired eyes against the glare, stepping around the fire to get a better look. But the figure was gone, blended once more into the darkness. "Hey, wait!"

Harvey turned to look about the camp, realizing he no longer heard his wife—her knocking and shouting had abated while he'd allowed his mind to wander. There was no sign of her now. He looked back toward the edge of camp, where just moments ago he'd seen that figure. "Dee?" he called. "Dee, are you out there?"

Shit, he couldn't see a thing out there! The firelight spoiled his eyes, and the stars seemed darker now—more distant than ever. Harvey debated a moment, then grabbed a bit of scrap wood from a nearby barrel. He wound one end with a bit of cloth he found on the ground, then plunged it into the fire, turning it into a makeshift torch. It wouldn't burn for long, but it was better than nothing. With this in hand he crossed to the edge of camp, stepping between the ramshackle dwellings and into the deeper dark beyond. The figure he'd seen was like a ghost, there and gone in an instant. But it couldn't have gone far.

"Hello!" Harvey called, sweeping the desert night with his torch. He stepped into the path he cut through the dark, the flickering torch leading the way. The dark closed greedily behind him, nipping at his heels.

Dee, he thought, *was that really you?*

In the desert ahead he expected to see only what he'd seen before: that endless, awful expanse of bone-colored rock and dust; Dee would be easy enough to spot on open ground, so long as she didn't get too far ahead. Dee...or whoever it was he'd seen by the fire. But instead of empty desert Harvey was met by a towering wall of dark stone. It ran on and on to his left and right. It might have been endless, might have gone on forever for all he knew. His light showed him precious little, and even that might have been too much; the wall appeared to move in the guttering light. The sight of it made him queasy.

There was no sign of Dee, or anyone else for that matter. But there was an opening in the wall just ahead, a jagged little cut that must have led into a narrow canyon. Harvey made for it, increasingly sure now that Dee hadn't come this way. He'd followed someone else out here, into the dark. But he kept on anyway, unwilling to turn back. He was driven by some irresistible urge to see, to *know*. Because that figure he'd seen by the fire...

No, that was just a trick of the light. It couldn't be real. Even here, in this world which had suddenly gone mad, some things were just too dreadful to believe.

The light showed the way, and Harvey followed it into the mouth of the canyon.

The walls closed in around him in an instant, shutting out the wider world. They pressed close, rose high overhead in dizzying, irregular towers. The light of his torch cast insane shadows that cavorted where they would, catching on corners, climbing into cracks. There were no stars here, not anymore. The rock devoured them all. Harvey tried to speak, but managed nothing but a wheeze. His lips were dry, his voice gone.

Still he moved forward, sweeping the torch ahead of him. The worms were here, as well. They wriggled out of the walls, crunching under the soles of his shoes as Harvey passed. Most were dead, but some were still alive. And some of these were substantially larger than the ones he'd seen before—better fed, perhaps. But what was there to eat out here in this wasteland? Harvey tried not to look at his grotesque company, tried to keep his eyes straight ahead. But he couldn't. There were fresh horrors to see. He was among the dead now.

Harvey dropped the torch. It fell at his feet as he stumbled backward with a gasp. The flame guttered and nearly went out in the dust, but it stayed lit just the same. It had to. Harvey needed to see what he'd found.

Empty sockets leered back at him from crevices in the rock, dead faces wasted and dried by the desert air. Some were fresh, others were ancient—faces out of time, faces from a different age—but they were all dead, lifeless, grinning things. Their bones were blackened. And the worms...

God, they were everywhere! Crawling, eating, sucking at those dry bones. They wriggled out of eye sockets, filled the cavities of hollow ribs. They pulsed with a fluid life all their own—life, where there should have been only death.

And there was more.

Harvey fell on his hands and knees in the dust, grabbing for the handle of his torch as he heard movement overhead. He jerked to his feet, spinning around to light the way, to see what he no longer wanted to see.

A figure appeared overhead. It crawled out of a grotto in the rock, followed closely by another, and another. They blotted out the night sky, peering down at him from where they'd nestled in the rock, dreaming whatever dark dreams such things may have. Harvey lifted his torch, screaming already, though he hadn't even seen the worst of it. Their bodies were hidden in ragged robes, their heads hooded. But the light showed their faces—not really faces at all but hungry pits, oozing spittle. Worms fell free of these hooded things, landing with a wet *splat* on the ground. They twisted about Harvey's feet, tied up in knots, coiled like spilled guts. Some fell upon his shoulder, heavier than they should have been for such small things, and cold—colder than death.

Harvey ran.

#

"Dee! *Dee!*" Harvey's voice was nothing to the desert air. He *tried* to scream; it was all he could think to do under the circumstances. Scream, and run. But the running took care of itself. His legs pumped with more power than he'd felt in decades—more life. Fear brought to his flesh and blood more vigor than any number of lifeless fucks, attention bought and paid for from desperate college girls. Fear told him he was alive. And fear told him he wanted to stay that way.

"Dee!" A little better this time, a little louder. But there was no one to greet him as he stumbled back into that rundown camp—neither his wife, nor those freaks he'd seen out there in the dark. The campfire still burned, but its light revealed nothing but dusty campers.

There was no sign of Dee.

Harvey fell to his hands and knees in the dust beside the fire. Jagged stones dug into his palms, but he hardly felt any pain. His lungs were burning. He had lost his torch somewhere along the way, but it hardly mattered now. He didn't want to see anymore.

He opened his mouth to call for Dee, to tell her they were *leaving,* goddammit. But a sound caught his voice in his throat, snagged it right there and held onto it. It wasn't his wife. Hell, it wasn't even those things he'd seen out there in the dark. This was a mundane sound–something he might have heard hundreds of times in his life. A sound that, more than any one thing, by its absence defined the rift that grew in his marriage.

It was the sound of a baby crying.

Harvey followed the sound to a dust-stricken single-wide trailer—the largest of the rundown shelters. His legs carried him there without being told. It was primal instinct all over again, not fear this time but something adjacent. He opened the rickety door and stepped inside.

The air hit him first: hot, stagnant. The kind of air that's hard to breathe. This was a place that had been shut up for some time, left to rot in the desert heat. But the impression faded just as quickly as it came. No, Harvey thought—this wasn't desert air at all. It was like he'd stepped into a different place entirely.

A different time.

Dee sat with her back to the door, in a chair Harvey knew, in a room he knew. It was a place from a past life: the nursery they had built for their baby. The baby that had, through no fault of its own, poisoned their marriage. The baby Harvey and Dee had, in their own separate ways, been running from ever since. The room hit Harvey like a punch in the gut.

He'd never wanted to see this place again. He'd had it stripped down to the walls, hadn't even done the work himself. How could he? That would have taken time—time he and Dee would have had to spend mourning the baby that never was—their daughter, their little girl. Neither of them could bear the thought of it.

And so they never mourned, never faced the truth—the room and what it meant. They drank and fought and shopped and fucked until the part of them that might have felt something—that *should* have felt something—was dead and gone.

Or so they thought.

But here it was, after all these years. The room and everything that came with it. Everything they had been running from.

"Harvey," Dee said. "Look."

He didn't want to. Didn't want to look, didn't want to *see*. But he saw it all just the same. The pastel colors, the crib, all those hopes and dreams sunk into this room they built and then unceremoniously destroyed. And the baby...

Harvey couldn't see it, not from where he stood by the door. Dee sat with her back to him, but she was turned in such a way that there was no mistaking what she held in her arms. It was in her posture, the pose and the care she took with that precious thing in her arms. Despite her faults—despite what they had both become since that day—there was never a doubt in Harvey's mind that Dee would have made an excellent mother.

And now...

Harvey stepped forward, though whether it was fear or wonder that moved him now he couldn't say. But either way he stepped with the greatest of care, measuring his steps so he wouldn't make a sound.

"I finally got her to quiet down," Dee said, her voice quiet, warmed through with affection Harvey hadn't heard in years. "She was crying something fierce when you went away."

Harvey rounded the back of the chair. The world slowed, seemed to hang in the balance. His every move threatened to push it over the edge. He felt drunk in the worst possible way—like the world was fragile, made of glass and much too *thin*, and he'd lost all control of himself. One wrong move and he'd fall through. Everything would shatter.

"Look."

He did, God help him, and what he saw swaddled there in Dee's lap *might* have been a doll. That would have been merciful. But this thing wasn't a doll, though the face that peered up at him from that nest of blankets in Dee's lap certainly resembled a doll's face—a pale visage like cracked porcelain, styled to mimic an infant's chubby features. But those were no doll's eyes in that varnished cherub's face. Black pits stared up at Harvey, empty, soulless wells that leaked oily, black ichor in a mockery of tears. Its mouth opened, revealing a twisting knot of worms. The thing cooed and the worms tumbled free of its open mouth, writhing with such force that the porcelain mask the thing boasted for a face split along its cracks.

Behind that mask was only wet, pulsing darkness.

Harvey fell backward, landing hard on his outstretched hands. He felt desert air at his back—dry and dusty. He smelled smoke from the fire outside. He gasped and got a lungful of stagnant air—shut-in air, like the inside of the trailer should have been all along.

The nursery was gone. Dee sat in a folding chair, facing a ratty old crib that was so busted up it might have been unwanted trash picked up along the side of the highway. The room presented nothing but dust and decay. This was no fit place for habitation—no place for a child. But Dee went on holding that bundle as if the thing that squirmed and wailed in her lap was her own.

A wonderful mother, indeed.

Harvey called out to her. He tried to get back on his feet, to put a stop to all this. But a hand on his shoulder pushed him back down. He wasn't surprised to see one of those awful hooded figures standing behind him. The shadows hid the face beneath that rotten hood, but Harvey knew what stared back at him. He could feel its gaze. It was disease, it was rot. It was death and grief and bitter, endless mourning and a thousand other things that no one wanted. It was a black, teeming pit that pulled and sucked, that would drag the heart down until there was no light.

It was an abyss.

Beneath that hood, Harvey saw something familiar—something he knew all too well. He saw himself. He saw a dead child, a dead marriage. He saw an ounce of misery that might have grown into something else, given time and attention; misery that might have *healed* but instead metastasized into something else. Something worse. Something hungry.

Harvey thought of the memorials that led them here, the pictures, the candles—shrines to all those black, bitter emotions. Emotions no one wanted, emotions that so often were exiled, thrown away like so much trash along the side of the road. But those shrines meant those emotions were attached to faces, lives, memories—and they had to go somewhere. What better place for exile than this miserable, barren place?

It was a place for lost, hungry things. A place for ghosts.

The hand on Harvey's shoulder was cold as death. It was heavy, impossible to get out from under. And there were more now, figures standing just outside the door. Harvey tried to scream, but the breath was snatched from his lungs. It left him empty, but the pain was still there, growing, blooming. And so very, very cold.

Dee, Harvey said—tried to say. But he had no voice. His lips were dry, his lungs empty. There was nothing in him now but the cold. *Stop. Please stop.*

But the sounds grew louder. The baby cooed, its brittle voice swelling into a cry of frustration and hunger. Dee did what she could to comfort it, shushing that little bundle of horror. But the thing in her lap did only what it knew how to do—what all babies did. It fed. And Dee, good mother that she was, did her job and fed the thing. Harvey could hear it. Stunned, silent, incapable of even doing as little as finding his feet, he could do nothing *but* hear it. The baby's hungry cries, Dee's whispered assurances—and then her screams—as that thing in her lap crawled its way to her throat and latched onto her flesh with a mouth made of hundreds of writhing, black worms.

It took what it needed, what nature demanded of it.

There were no more screams after that.

#

The sun burned Harvey's eyes. He raised one hand against it; his other hand cradled something heavy against his chest. The road opened before him, two lanes of weary blacktop baking in the desert sun. Harvey could feel the heat coming up from the ground. It was like standing in an oven. The sensation was familiar. He'd walked this road before, just...

When was that, exactly? He was having a hard time remembering. But he knew the way, he knew the road—this miserable, heat-blasted hellscape. And that was his car just ahead, pulled off onto the shoulder, gleaming like white fire in the sun. It was just where he left it. But he hadn't been alone, had he? A thought stirred, something deep and murky. Something dredged up from where it lay hidden. And a feeling spread with it, something cold in Harvey's chest. Something heavy, lonely. Like a hole in his heart.

Dee, he thought. He felt his gut turn over. And then he looked down.

The baby stared up at him from where it lay, cradled against Harvey's chest. There was a moment of horror, an instant of blood-chilling revulsion that came from somewhere else—a dream, perhaps. Because certainly Harvey could never fear this bundle of joy in his arms, his precious little girl. She stared up at him with those pretty blue eyes; naturally, she favored her mother. What a pair they made.

"Are you hungry?" Harvey asked. The baby cooed, squirming in her swaddling clothes.

Of course she was hungry. Harvey looked to his free hand, at the wounds that had only just begun to close: tooth marks, sucked clean of blood. He put his wrist to his daughter's mouth.

She was always hungry.

THE FIELD TRIP
Matt Neil Hill

AKA: The Experimental Therapies of
Mr. Sweet and Dr. Gore

Mr. **Sweet** is *contagious.*

And, in his contagion, he is searching for something. A place to feel at home, I think. Perhaps his *actual* home, though no such place was mentioned in his records. A town, but more than that: a specific street; a house; a *room.* Impossible to know at this stage, but then we have barely begun our quest, our healing crusade. He is not an easy man to help, but that is my job. *My calling.*

From the safety of the driving seat, I follow his implacable progress across the deserted forecourt to settle the debt for the gas we have just pumped—his pockets rattling, though not with coins. Hiding birds and insects chirp in response. The reek of smoke, junk food and unwashed bodies fills the car even with the windows down. Not the Mercedes, of course. No, *that's* now a fire-gutted shell under a flyover half a dozen counties back; fetal-positioned corpse in the trunk with its teeth knocked out and hands amputated, my cell phone melted to slag somewhere in the wreckage. Today it's a dust-colored Chevy Caprice that Mr. Sweet took a liking to outside a bar I can't remember the name of. I get the impression he used to own one. The radio is broken, disappointingly. One of the many things this journey needs is music: external soundtrack versus internal monologue to either soothe or energize the mind. Silence can be revealing, but too much of it is unproductive, cannibalistic.

The lights above Mr. Sweet are brighter than an operating theater; brighter even than the glare I've heard about once or twice from near-deathers. I light a cigarette, knowing I'm not supposed to this close to so much flammable material. Just one of the many things I'm meant to have quit, but recently I've been trying hard to live a less rigid existence. Calista—my third and possibly-still-current wife—will be *furious* if she ever smells it on me.

To be honest, it's something of a relief she isn't here.

Restless, I worry at my necktie, throat constricted and sore from its grip. The knot is stubborn. It grinds against my nasal cartilage as I pull it over my head, and I realize for the first time in years how much the thing resembles a noose: if only one that professional decorum dictates. I'm off the clock—from one perspective at least—and I don't have to wear it anymore if I don't want to. I think it had become a talisman, one that I no longer need. Made of silk, maroon with a hound's-tooth pattern: a birthday present from Calista, one of many beautiful yet utterly impersonal gifts on some birthday or other special occasion. I toss it out the window and suck in the vibrantly cold night air; it tastes of Christmas and gasoline.

I adjust the rear-view, but with too much force. The face I see is smaller than my thumb nail and pinned to my chest, though still my own. My crumpled suit is the color of the sea in those final inches before all light disappears, my shirt the soiled white of dubious haloes. I look at my watch, but it's gone. No, not gone: simply on the wrong wrist, for reasons that escape me. My father's. The spoils of war, pillaged in the aftermath of alleged bravery. In its customary spot there is a plasticized hospital bracelet with my name and a number sequence in something almost like my own handwriting. The bracelet tells the same story as the badge.

Gore.

I am *Dr.* Gore.

First do no harm, they teach us. As either a motto or instruction, I always felt that it was both trite and open to interpretation. To do no harm, in any branch of medicine, verges on the impossible. How would one excise the tumor without slicing through perfectly healthy tissue? How would one cure psychological trauma without pushing the patient, however gently, to relive it over and over again?

Every treatment has its associated pain, its side effect.

Still, I think of the mutilated body in the Mercedes. Mr. Sweet's first victim in nearly forty years, and us not even out of the hospital grounds. One of the younger security staff, in enough debt for my bribe to gain us the right keys and a blind CCTV eye. I had cautioned Mr. Sweet not to do what he did, but I'm sure in the eyes of the law that would make me no less culpable. Mr. Sweet teaching me a valuable lesson about trust, leading to cash purchases of a hammer and hacksaw at separate hardware stores.

David.

I think the security guard's name was David.

I stare at my ID badge. A younger version of me, and cleaner cut. A lifetime ago, yet made up of so few hours in the grand scheme of things.

I readjust the mirror for a second opinion. The reflected face matches the photograph, although my skin is more yellow and the sclera of my eyes greyer than I recall. The last handful of days have been challenging, undertaken at a sub-optimal level of health. I smooth down my mousy, greasy hair, and smoke my next-to-last cigarette. My tongue is a salted slug, my lungs the morning-after charcoal of a house fire. Littered across the dashboard are a hundred and one transparent orange pill bottles, the contents in various stages of consumption. I sift through them and make my selections.

A noise: short, sharp, and not too far away. The creatures of the night go still. I turn towards the gas station. The lights beneath the canopy seem so intense, barely less damaging than gazing directly at an eclipse. Tears come. Photosensitivity from the pills no doubt. The building beyond is almost a mirage, a pale watercolor rendition of an actual place, impressionistic almost to the point of being unrecognizable. There are windows, glass that will flow to earth over a long enough axis of time. Beyond these are displayed the spectral dolls of trapped souls, some of whom move and some of whom do not. I assume the one most like a praying mantis must be Mr. Sweet. I continue to watch this late-night TV spectacle, this part-scripted reality show, as I open the bottles by feel and tip out the desired dosages by intuition. Tiny capsules of micro-and macro-adjustment stick to the roof of my mouth. I trawl the detritus in the footwells and dredge up a bottle with a couple of sips of water remaining.

Drink.

Swallow.

Breathe.

To have brought Mr. Sweet on the road like this is a risk—although not primarily, I believe, for me. It simply became unethical to wait any longer. Were my immediate colleagues or the State Board feeling especially charitable, I believe they would class the treatment program I have devised as *unorthodox.* It *is,* of course, but no more so than is required. Their lack of understanding is not my problem—although it may still become one—but when the end of a road is reached it is sometimes necessary to relocate from the metaphorical plane to the literal. Physical and chemical restraints are not the be-all and end-all. Talking therapies can become circular, masturbatory. What is required to move forward may, on rare and very special occasions, be more experiential in nature. What's essential is a level of courage most contemporary clinicians lack.

Hence our field trip, our dalliance outside the asylum walls.

Another of those percussive, painful little noises rings out; tortuous, expectant moments after the first. I shake my head. The forecourt illuminations perish a moment or two later. I swear I can almost feel my pupils blossoming, filaments of muscle obeying my brain's insistence on the need to capture more light. A breeze arrives like a sigh drifting over from another country, barely sufficient to ruffle the needles on the surrounding pines, carrying with it the smell of hot metal and entropy.

I look at my watch, its beetle-black hands sluggish against the pearlescent dial. After ninety dragging seconds the lights inside the gas station go out too. No luminosity remains but the silvering tide of the moon's unconditional love for the earth. The stars are up there too, cloaked by the lingering pollution of dead fluorescents, biding their excess of time. Traces of their ancient radiation soak into my pores, realign the mercury in my teeth.

I light a new cigarette from the old, send the butt on the same journey as the necktie. The crumpled pack joins a dozen others in the stew of trash at my feet, not yet quite deep enough to bury skeletons.

The gas station door opens. Mr. Sweet's silhouette emerges, tendrils of lank hair writhing around his shoulders, raw-boned body flowing with determined grace towards the Chevy, drawn towards the glowing coal at my lips.

I am a beacon for him in the dark.

He clutches a large paper sack in each hand. He is a shadow among shadows, flickering, born of the world's troubled sleep. Beneath the lightless canopy the suit he wears appears black, but I know it to be oxblood. It's an antique, a mothballed reliquary he had not been permitted to wear for well over three decades before I arrived on the scene. It still fits him perfectly, not an ounce added to or subtracted from that spare frame over the years of his incarceration. As far as I know, the tongues and ears and areolas found in his pockets when arrested still adorn some evidence locker somewhere, perhaps refrigerated or else dried over the many years to bitter jerky. He wears no accompanying shirt or tie, no shoes. I have never seen him exhibit a moment's discomfort when walking over gravel or the twinkling peek of broken glass amidst soft green grass, his feet calloused by time and cracked hospital tiles. Mr. Sweet is more than adequately armored against the world's barbs. As he steps out beneath the moon's cabaret spotlight there are murky spots across his cheek and a flat, soporific cast to his eyes.

When he reaches the car, he sets one of his packages down on the ground and opens the rear door, then tosses the other into the back seat. It lands there with a wet thud, settling with a soft crackle of brown paper. I experience the future ghost of Calista's disapproving sigh. He slams one door and opens the other, slides down into the passenger seat without a sound. The cuffs of his jacket are soaked almost black, his protruding hands a bright, shining, sticky red. Arterial Morse code sprayed across his cheek and forehead the same shade. He sits very precisely within the aura of the dome light's tallow glow, the remaining sack balanced on his angular thighs, and stares straight ahead, his lips sealed.

When I was introduced as one of his new physicians, his first—and so far only—word to me was *"finally."* Eyebrows in the room were raised, and notes amended. Mr. Sweet, the forgotten demon languishing in his archaic hole, saw something in me that turned his lonely world on its head. And what followed for those who had been *treating* him all those years was the unbearable cacophony of a rare breaking of silence.

I had arrived at that institution by virtue of some minor breakthroughs with other forensic cases; those who, until alarmingly recently, had been referred to as the criminally insane. Men—and they are almost invariably men—who had committed the most heinous of crimes yet were spared lethal injections and equally fatal chairs because of their malfunctioning brains. Occasionally the end result of my interventions had been remorse, but more often than not all I had done was drag the homicidal far enough back out of their psychotic fog for the penal system to declare them fit for either execution of standard imprisonment. Mr. Sweet, with all his voiceless inscrutability, was something of a challenge.

He had grown weary, over the better and worse part of a near half-century, of the same old questions. In my defence, I suppose I had likewise grown fatigued with pale imitations of the same answer. I had tried for months to elicit a verbal response from him, my patience unrewarded within that succession of over-lit, ammonia-scented, scarred-plaster rooms. Chained at wrist and ankle to a chair bolted to the floor, his deep-sea predator stare remained the only sign that he noticed me at all during those initial weeks. I could not help but feel the chill of his disappointment in me, my failure to realise whatever potential he had seen in that initial meeting. My colleagues laughed behind my back. Implied that I was not so special after all. But not one of them was willing to admit, as I was, that as a profession we place too much emphasis on the *linguistic* expression of our psychic mechanisms, be they aberrant or otherwise.

And so, despite his relapse into selective mutism, we *do* manage to communicate.

I cough quietly as he sits in the passenger seat with that sack balanced on his legs. After a few seconds he clucks his tongue in mild annoyance and reaches inside his jacket. Pulls out the revolver he plucked from an overtired state trooper's holster three days ago and places it back in the glove box. He has become remarkably adept at removing the thing without me noticing. I have as yet been unable to convince him to part with any of his knives.

He reclines and resumes his vigil. I leave him to process while I concentrate on the growing flush of the latest medicating cocktail beneath my skin, the placid warmth of it in my bones. A collision of dopamine agonists, SSRIs and anxiolytics—a trial I know to be unsustainable in the long run but pleasing enough for now. Experimentation rules our kingdom. There are potential pitfalls, but this is true of almost any endeavor. Platitudes I've crooned to patients and their families in the past have, to my surprise, become undeniable truth.

It is important to feel happy and calm.

It is essential to be in control.

The end justifies the means.

I dismiss the memory of sitting in a rest stop bathroom stall trying to control the tremor in my hands, aftershocks of the effort taken to saw through David's wrists. Mr. Sweet had insisted on removing the teeth.

He requires nothing to salve his conscience; for me, carbamazepine and magnesium have dulled the outward signs of any guilt.

Nothing will be achieved here though, if I am unable to focus on the necessary interpretations of Mr. Sweet's behaviors. I smoke my cigarette, exhaling all cancerous judgements as I observe.

His ashen hair is knotted and untameable. The positioning of his limbs so much like a storefront mannequin: stiff, exaggerated, and posed in echo of someone else's idea of how a normal human being should behave. Slow and even respiration. I cannot tell from my angle whether he gazes at his own reflection in the windshield or studies the lunar-lit landscape beyond the glass: the tarmac and the pines, the capricious stars; or perhaps some interstitial realm of existence whose wavelength only he can divine. However long this little jaunt of ours is allowed to continue, I fear I will never fully unpack the man's mind. I worry equally that there is no substance inside his skull beyond his lizard brain, and that I and every psychiatrist before me has merely been projecting our own desolate fantasies and failures onto a blank screen.

Mr. Sweet is *opaque.*

Mr. Sweet is *fractal.*

Mr. Sweet is, as I said, *contagious.*

He watches me in the uncaring night. The temperature around me drops further, gooseflesh prickling at the nape of my neck and across my scalp. In a rare moment of doubt, I remind myself he is just a man, his damaged psyche deformed further by institutionalization. I advise my face to smile back and it does what it's told, after a moment. He dips stained hands into his package of gas station trinkets. He fans a wad of grubby bills at me, somehow aware that the withdrawal from my and Calista's shared accounts, though substantial, will likely not last long enough to complete his treatment.

He passes me a pack of cigarettes—unfiltered, anachronistic, and not my brand but rather the one my father smoked his whole life, even as tumors spread languorously from his lungs to his temporal lobes, dragging his ability to verbalize thoughts through the mud of profanity and incoherence in those final months. The words of approval I'd grown middle-aged waiting to hear remained unspoken by that point, due to actual deletion from his vocabulary rather than the stubbornness and meanness of spirit presiding before. Calista tried her best to soothe me through that difficult time, and I pretended to her that she'd succeeded, unable to find harm in the lie.

I am reasonably certain I've never divulged a single one of these facts or recollections to Mr. Sweet at any point. If his records are correct, he was born the same year as my father—and I *wholeheartedly* refute the obvious psychodynamic interpretations of *this* fact—so perhaps it's a brand he recognized with a sense of nostalgia, even though he could have easily brought me the one I have repeatedly told him I prefer. I accept what he offers, not wishing to appear ungrateful.

His smile widens.

His second gift is a tall can of some hyper-caffeinated soda, the logo embossed on aluminium as black as the occulted sky. I trace my thumb over the condensation-slicked letters, but the font is so convoluted I still have no idea of its name. It is doubtless something suitably macho, befitting a substance designed to bludgeon me awake. Mr. Sweet selects a family-sized bag of candy for himself. Tears it open and pours in a bottle of a medication designed for children with a condition he doesn't have, in order to ensure he will not sleep. According to his notes even Mr. Sweet sleeps, though I have not witnessed it myself. That *I* have slept on our journey demonstrates the extent of the trust that exists between us. Or, perhaps, more realistically, the trust *I* have placed in *him*. We are still together. I am not dead.

He stirs the candy and drugs with a sticky finger. The sound is like the tooth fairy rattling its overnight bag.

I pull our road map from the door pocket and unfold it on my lap. The scale allows for the names of places I never would have known existed; populations measured by the handful. Backwoods places where the second hand of history runs slow and the pharmacies will not stock the drugs we need, no matter how many prescriptions I write nor how loudly I protest their absolute necessity for a successful outcome.

No one there will care who or what I am.

This may not be the worst thing under the circumstances, however much it pricks my pride. There is a certain hollow thrill to be had in imagining what may happen when these hundred and one bottles are empty, like probing the gaping socket of a swallowed tooth, metallic juices sharp against the tongue. I wonder what folk remedies we might be compelled to entertain when our minds are left to their own unfiltered chemical devices. Recent research has highlighted the success of LSD micro-dosing in the treatment of depressive patients, although I'm certain neither of us are depressed. I stare at the lines of inked asphalt dissecting the map. In an unprecedented level of doctor-patient collaboration, it is my turn to choose our next port of call. I pull a damp shred of tobacco from my lower lip—both sweet and bitter, like the seed of some exotic and decaying fruit—and allow my eyes to lose focus. I feel Mr. Sweet shift toward me, the shape of his will filling the small space, pushing me on. I let go. My fingertip slides dry across the miniature world, godlike destroyer of forest and swamp, settlement and lake. The destination is relatively unimportant to us: what matters is what we learn along the way. And what we feed our bodies to get us there.

My finger stops and I look down. Mr. Sweet leans in closer to see my selection. He grunts, and in my peripheral vision I note the shrug of his shoulders and the smile that unstitches itself across his lips. Have I spontaneously discovered something? I wonder if he has been to this place before. If survivors—should any exist—would remember him. I look forward to discovering if he or they will find the strength to make amends.

This is *the work.*

I snap my lighter shut and refold the map, the cigarette between my lips threatening to burn my face. When I have a hand free, I pluck it out and eject it from the car. I turn to him against the sickening gravitational pull of the thing in the back seat.

"We're going to have to *talk* about all this, you know" I say, nodding behind me. "Sooner or later."

Mr. Sweet rotates his face in my direction, but his smile is gone. His eyes are deep pits, devoid of expression. There is a tension in his skin, in the particles of matter between us. I have stared him down before: in therapy groups, in the fetid cell of his room. I am not afraid of him, for better or worse. Not really. I believe there is a mutual respect. After a minute or an hour, he shrugs again and turns his face away, resumes delving into his bag of rainbow colored sugar and methylphenidate. He doesn't swallow until there exists a mass large enough to make his throat bulge. I turn the key in the ignition and the lights cut through the darkness. I eye the second sack he brought back from the gas station. What it conceals rests like a huge egg; the rich, thick, crimson stain spreading through the paper onto the upholstery accompanied by the aroma of coppery meat and stillborn thoughts.

Somewhere in the world, Calista shudders without knowing why. She so *detests* mess. I never minded it myself, but my gut instinct—the one she's transferred to me by operant conditioning, years of brandishing coasters and straightening my bookshelves to the accompaniment of clicking teeth and sucked breath—is to discard the package, but that would be to skip a step in Mr. Sweet's assessment. For the sake of convention this grisly keepsake should form part of our discussion, but it may merely be ornamentation for the journey, of no more significance to him than a boggle-eyed window plush. Or a splash of color on an otherwise dull excursion.

I let it be, for now.

Focus on the way ahead.

Such a course of action is *liberating*.

The stars begin to emerge as we drive away, inverted votive pinpricks above the forest's jagged cathedral spires. The wind through the windows hushes us needlessly as we pick up speed. My lungs and stomach must be scoured by tar and taurine, but I barely feel them now through the pharmaceutical miasma. Physical sensations and mental constructs begin to dissolve. The path before us is possessed of both pleasant vagaries and dreadful clarity. I must evolve as a healer in order to manage my patient's pain, his wordless outward expressions of inner torment.

He had been locked away for so very long—though not, I will admit, without cause. It has fallen to me to transform him because no one in his life before now has had the insight or the inclination. Except— nothing *fell*. I *chose* this. Would do so again. I have nothing to prove; yet everything. I tilt my head to watch him as we cruise, his oily grey curls like Medusa's serpents rearing through the open window as he surveys the night and turns all tiny watching feral eyes to stone. Reluctantly, I return my attention to the road.

The world unspools. We move deeper into the trees between us and the next point on the map. Faces extrude from the gnarled bark as we flash past; nightmares waving us down with the serrated gulf between their beckoning wooden hands. Small rocks and potholes shiver. The roar of a full tank stains the air. I inhale the decadent scent of apothecary-sated bodies at rest. Somewhere ahead lie myriad tiny escapes, a billion subtly different alternate universes for us to inhabit.

I see them *all*.

The one in which we devour a succession of isolated gas stations and small communities, eventually rolling into the ocean in search of treasures more primordial than mere earth and concrete can offer.

The one where we preside over a flock of the damaged and deranged, praying by firelight to the putrefying, fly-girdled contents of the paper sack beneath giggling, ravenous heavens.

The one in which I awake one morning to the insistent tap of a patrolman's baton against the glass on which I rest my head, Mr. Sweet nowhere to be seen, and the stench of rot from the back seat to be explained along with the tell-tale hospital bracelet at my wrist.

Another where Calista never sees me again and grows old in safe seclusion, but is never again at ease.

One where key components of her abandoned body and mind travel with us in the trunk, wrapped in sackcloth and silk; little parcels of dental enamel and stripped alveoli, forlorn hopes and dead dreams.

Another where I sob against the cold lip of a motel tub, Mr. Sweet's unfathomable, unfixable brain spongiform between my fingers as a result of the impromptu surgery he eventually permits me to perform when even he is jaded and out of ideas, his unnameable thoughts trapped screaming in the stained mirror above the sink.

Yet another where it is I who twitches in the bath of blood and spinal fluid, having made of him the same exhausted request, my head leaking his contagion and the mirror filled with nothing but the fathomless dark.

Endless.

The possibilities are *endless*.

My life's work. *Our* life's work.

But... I... *drift*.

I look at my watch, the one inherited from a man of war. He never would have considered me worthy of it, and he was right. I've fought in no battle he'd recognize. I wrestled the thing from my father's wrist when he was radiation-addled and festering in his own shit, as much because I wanted him to be without it at the end as any feeling it should be mine. A sharpness came into his opiate gaze as I took it, a look of combined fear and loathing I had perhaps seen before. He did not look surprised, that's for sure. He must have known I would take it from him one day, but he was no prophet. Fuck him, though: it's just a watch. The temporal is dead out here. I unfasten the strap with my teeth and toss it to the void. At this velocity, by the time it lands I have traveled too far to hear the shattering of glass or the tinkling of its spilled workings. I suck the wedding band from my finger and spit it into the night. Tear off my staff ID and launch it into the blurring forest. My teeth are not equal to the fabric of the hospital bracelet, and so it stays. This is who I am now.

The stars smear and explode as I accelerate, far too many for me to count.

I light another cigarette and suck down the flames, burning with exhilaration.

This is why I became a doctor. This—this—*unfettered* experience of another, a genuine immersion in holism, a rejection of existing theory for a remaking of the self, his and mine. How *can* the self be perfected without laying itself entirely bare?

How?

The road is an epileptic snake, endlessly regurgitating its auto-cannibalized flesh; jittering black diamonds, halogen bright, reddened by burst-apart fox and jackrabbit beneath our wheels, tail light inferno in our wake. My foot heavy on the gas the fir trees shimmer, ghost-green, waxing and waning as we climb and dive across mountainsides, the path forever ahead, no point in retracing our steps. My knuckles crack around the wheel. One second abyssal darkness and the next a solar flare that takes my breath away: a child gasping at the firework display of his own overloading brain. Scorched tires, slipping and sliding; the package in the back seat thrown heavy and wet against my seat back, *complainant;* the bite of Mr. Sweet's unbitten nails in the crook of my right arm. The brake pedal beneath my sole, the Caprice fishtailing in a question mark of dust and gravel, shocks groaning, the lament of the inanimate in terminated motion. The engine dead, we sit and wait, positioned at the edge of a drop-off, nothing but the night beneath us.

I turn my face to him, feeling the arctic night air against the front of my bared teeth and the hot black gusting of my overworked lungs against the back. He relaxes his grip on me, but not the sternness in his lips, his brows.

Am I getting through to him at last?

"Not ready to die yet?" I ask. "Good. *Good.*"

He puts his red hand back in his lap. Perhaps the flicker of a smile; a simulacrum of admiration, of recognition. The tang of burned rubber drifts through the windows. I look past Mr. Sweet to a scarred metal sign on a pole. A town, named after some place or person in some long-dead Puritan's bible. *Population 87.* I can't remember if this is the place my finger chose, but what does that matter?

Too many *rules.*

I listen to the night; to the distant zephyr sighing of the wind, the hammering of tiny heartbeats and the hooting of owls. Already over-stimulated I crack open the can Mr. Sweet gave me and suck down the contents. It tastes of fruit grown in a crack lab and has the consistency of phlegm. Warm as my own body, my own mouth—and how *long* was I driving? My eyes and hands doing the work of my brain as it frolicked in some other vertiginous space.

I light a new cigarette, try the ignition. The engine turns over and I roll the car up the incline. Over the peak the town flickers in the depths below. A handful of streets, of houses, lives. Small and cossetted on its lumber-stripped plateau, safe in the moon's phosphorescence before we arrive. Patient and doctor. Doctor and patient. With our medicines and bone-sharpened knives and gasoline. Our prescriptions. Mr. Sweet's and Dr. Gore's odyssey spread out before them like a chart of enlightenment decipherable only by the cartographers themselves, of no use to the remaining living or the increasing tally of dead.

Population 87.

What number will adorn that tired old sign a week from now?

I try not to waste the moment speculating over who will be my next David; desperate to be helpful, drenched in gasoline, raw-gummed and unable to applaud my achievements, waiting for the scrape of my lighter's flint.

I press down with my foot, but softly now.

As we begin the newest phase of our descent, and with a voice not of the angels, Mr. Sweet begins to hum a fragment of song I do not recognize. The melody is cracked and primitive, dissonantly soothing in its own way. We *are* to provide our own music it seems. The refrain loops, each note duplicated with precision and affection.

As I say, I do not know the lullaby he sings.

But I sense that I will learn it, somewhere not too far along the road.

And we will sing it together, until the very end.

RIDERS ON THE STORM
Charlotte Vale

Weary pavement sliced through the dense Cascade Forest, stretching into a gray horizonless sky. Hoof beats driven by an early September storm thundered through low dark clouds, drawing a cold, stiff wind after them.

Giant pines, firs, and spruce whispered over the girl as she walked. *Shhh*. She drew her oversized coat tighter around her and sang softly to herself a song she heard four years ago outside a little white, high-steepled church in Ritzville.

The hoof beats grew louder over her, and she lifted her face to the dark heavens. A swollen drop of rain broke against her cheek. One drop became three, and then a dozen, slapping at her body, bursting against the pavement. A dozen swollen drops became a torrent, battering her small, hunched frame. There was shelter beneath the thick bows of the trees, but she trudged on, thinking only of home. Home, where the sun shone warm on a crumbling walk. On tufts of green, pushing through the cracks, reaching for the sky. And a rock in her hand drew flowers, and trees, and happy little houses on the cement.

She sagged beneath the weight of the black leather coat as it greedily drank in the rain. She got the coat off a carnie in Puyallup the previous fall. While she devoured barbecued chicken, and coleslaw, and buttered corn on the cob, he bragged about stealing it from some drunk in a bar. It matched the black cowboy boots she took from a cowboy in Lewiston the year before. He fancied himself an outlaw, a real rough guy. She took his black hat as well. Her stomach was empty that night. And her eye was swollen shut.

Now, rain poured off the brim of the hat, down her back, and the boots, too large for her feet, were small wading pools, sloshing with each step.

Her peasant skirt clung wet and cold to her legs, leeching her body heat. But she didn't mind. She'd had the skirt and blouse longest of all; the day she found them was the happiest day of her life. Tie-dyed bursts of yellow and blue, colliding into the brightest green. She imagined the woman who'd worn them, tall, slender, beautiful. She imagined a man had given them to the woman, but he hurt her, so she threw them away. Threw *him* away.

The skirt was long on her, but when she knotted the waistband, it sat securely enough on the ledge of her bony hips. It was that same day, that same dumpster, where she'd found the kiddy meal, all boxed up and waiting for her. There was only one bite out of the cheeseburger—she loved cheeseburgers—and most of the fries were there, the soda only half-gone. Hearing the music from the little white church, she'd carried her treasures to the front steps of the church. As she sat, washing cold fries down with watery soda, she found it, still sealed in plastic. A miniature princess. Her daddy had called her his princess.

She freed the princess from her plastic prison and pressed a button, sending her twirling on a pedestal to the music seeping through the pretty colored windows of the church. They were singing the song— the song she sang, now.

There's power in the blood, power in the blood.

In that moment she knew. She had a fairy godmother, just like the little princess. There was no beautiful woman or cruel man; her fairy godmother had brought her all these wonderful gifts. It was then, sitting on the steps of the little white church, she was reborn. Her fairy godmother had set her free—just as she had sent the girl to free the little princess from her own prison. She'd made up her mind then. October first was her new birthday.

Her steps now slowed at the incline of the road. She lowered the brim of the hat against the deluge and pressed on through the *shhh* of the rain. Her grip tightened on the little princess in her pocket at the sound of an engine approaching behind her. She didn't stop, didn't look back.

A white, windowless van drove past her and crackled to a stop on the gravel shoulder, its brake lights two amber beacons in the gray afternoon. Her pace remained slow and steady as she approached the van, her fingers tracing the rusty orange gash running its length before opening the passenger door.

"Where ya headed?" The driver, dented and rusty as his van, dwarfed behind the steering wheel. He had the appearance of a man whose balding head was sinking gradually into his midsection.

"As far as you can take me," she said, climbing into the passenger seat.

His smile was a derelict graveyard, tombstones, broken and blackened, or absent altogether. She turned away from him to empty the rain from her boots before pulling the door closed. She would be home soon. Home, where sunlight broke through the edges of drawn shades, turning dancing bits of dust into diamonds, setting swirling cigarette smoke aglow.

Her legs and hands all the colder in the warmth of the van, she drew her arms around her trembling body. A bright green rabbit's foot swung from the keychain in the ignition. She didn't need luck. She had a fairy godmother. But the rabbit's foot matched the green in her skirt.

"Nasty weather." The short fat man's gaze rolled down her form, coming to rest on her legs. "I'll turn up the heat for ya." He adjusted the knobs on the dash and steered onto the pavement. "You may want to take that wet coat off." She watched him shift in his seat as she pulled her arms free of the wet leather, the rise and fall of his round belly quickening. "You like The Doors?"

She nodded, laying the coat on the seat between them.

He mopped his broad forehead with a flannel sleeve before thrusting an 8-track tape into the slot. She'd seen one like it in the truck of one of her daddy's friends. "Classic," the man called it, handing her a small, stinky cigarette. Her daddy didn't like music. He didn't let her smoke his cigarettes. But her daddy wasn't there. He told her he would buy her a cake when she got home that day. It was her eighth birthday, the second of September. When his friend brought her back home, he handed her daddy a twenty-dollar bill. She was dizzy, and sore—and so hungry. While her daddy drank beer and smoked with his friend on the front porch, she took a loaf of white bread and a jar of peanut butter into her room. She knew she would get the belt, but she didn't care. She devoured the whole loaf, licked the last of the peanut butter from her fingers, and fell asleep in the darkness of her empty closet. She never got a cake.

The heat of the van pulled at her, despite the rising odor that reminded her of a supermarket dumpster. Through weighted lids she watched the short fat man's gaze dart from her breasts to the road ahead and back, the crotch of his dirty jeans growing tighter. The van rocked gently as she drifted off to a rhythmic *clack, clack, clack* somewhere behind her and the voice of Jim Morrison.

Come on, baby, light my fire...

She woke to the thunder of hooves and the sting of bleach in her nose. The sting reminded her of Puyallup, the carnie and his glass pipe. The van was no longer moving. Beyond the smoke-filled cab and the bug-spattered windshield, a wall of green swayed in the wind, like the weeping willow in the front yard back home. It was so close, now. The thunder coming from stereo speakers was joined by a vibrating bass and the melodic tripping of fingers down an electric keyboard.

"Have a nice nap?" The short fat man licked his flaky lips again, stashing his glass pipe under his seat. He mopped his face with the plaid shirt he was no longer wearing and kneaded his thigh. "You're not gonna give me any trouble, now, are ya?"

Riders on the storm...

Wiry orange hairs wriggled at the edges of his grimy wifebeater as his chest heaved.

She shook her head.

He exposed a graveyard smile and jerked at the curtains to the back of the van. "Get on back there and lose the dress."

Into this world we're thrown...

She did as she was told, the stench of rot greeting her beyond the curtain. A mattress filled the space between the wheel wells, its dark stains refusing to be concealed beneath the wrinkled, threadbare sheet despite the dim light. The van rocked with her movement. *Clack, clack, clack,* went the handcuffs hanging from the side panels. An oil rag dangled from a hole in the back door where the handle should have been. The smell of it reminded her of her daddy—and home. Home, where the thick, black night, smelling of sweat, motor oil, and Jim Beam, pressed down on her, smothering her in her bed.

Her breathing slowed, deepened.

There's a killer on the road...

She watched the short fat man's eyes in the rearview mirror as she peeled the wet skirt down her legs. She heard him lap hungrily at his crusted lips as she rolled it up and tucked it in the backpack she'd taken from a college boy in Corvallis—a real smart guy. She pulled off the blouse, feeling the chill that had begun to fill the van, and lastly her white panties, adding them to the pack. She laid back on the mattress as the short fat man climbed clumsily through the curtains. She raised her knees, as he kneeled on the mattress.

"You gonna die with your boots on, cowgirl?"

She watched the slight swelling in his pants shrink away, and she knew what was coming.

He worked at the buckle beneath his generous gut, and when he'd managed to lower his pants, his predicament became obvious to him as well. He glared down at her, his face a glowing red coal, and then lunged, striking her hard across her mouth. Her head snapped to the side, reverberating from the blow. The garbage around her took form as the pain ebbed, her gaze landing on a tooth with four brown-flaked roots. She turned back to him, probing the swelling gash in her lip with her tongue, tasting her own salt. He flashed his graveyard smile again. It had only taken the one blow to revive him.

"You don't even put up a fight, do ya?" His hand closed around her throat as he came down on her, hot breath like the grave. She could see the front door of home, now, with its peeling blue paint.

Girl, you gotta love your man...

Her hand slid down her leg and into her boot as he grunted and jerked against her. Her palm closed around the key that would let her through that blue door, and she drew it out.

Penetration was effortless, barely noticeable. Her breath caught when it had gone its length. Another grunt from him sent electricity surging through her body, igniting explosions of pleasure in her head. She drew the blade upward with ease, as if she were drawing it through water—along the ribcage—stopping abruptly at his sternum. She had taken the hunting knife from her daddy four years ago. That was on her thirteenth birthday, and it was the last time she saw her daddy alive.

The short fat man rose over her, eyes wide in horror and disbelief, sending a rush of hot crimson and intestine slithering over her naked skin.

She drew the rich, coppery odor of life deep into her lungs, growing lighter with each breath.

"You *bitch*," he spat.

But she had gone by then. She had stepped through that door with the peeling blue paint.

Riders on the storm...

He collapsed on her in a quivering heap, an inhuman groan gurgling up in his throat. A warm crimson stream issued from his parted lips, snaking its way down her glistening neck, pooling in her matted hair, seeping through the sheet, down into the waiting mattress.

She wrapped her arms around him, breathing heavily into his greasy orange hair, stroking it gently. Tears rolled hot and heavy into her ears and hair as the notes of the organ danced to the rumble of retreating hooves. Outside, the rain had stopped.

"Shhh," she whispered. "It's all right, Daddy. I've come home again." She kissed his cool, damp forehead as he convulsed, gave one last rattling gasp, and went still.

#

Storm clouds gathered in the September sky over the Blue Mountains as the girl crested the hill overlooking Pendleton. The town bustled with local and out-of-town revelers kicking off the festivities of the Pendleton Round Up. She drew the brim of her hat down against the rising wind, but for now, her leather coat remained stowed neatly in her backpack. The bright green rabbit's foot now hanging from the knot in her tie-dyed skirt, bounced rhythmically to the scrape of her oversized boots against the pavement. She sang softly to herself as she walked:

There's power in the blood, power in the blood...

MASTER OF THE HOUSE
Mark Wheaton

"**We should** be pouring asphalt!" Watkins complained, sun beating down on the unfinished interstate. "Asphalt cools fast! Pour it. Do two passes with a steam roller. It's ready for cars in twenty minutes!"

Vilmos smiled as he smoothed the edges of the recently poured concrete slab with his trowel. If Watkins was already delivering his daily asphalt monologue, it wouldn't be long before the chuck wagon arrived with lunch.

"What do you have against concrete?" Vilmos asked, playing his part even as his Hungarian accent made the word sound like "conkrit." "It's strong. It's stable. It lasts."

"You have to coddle concrete!" Watkins replied, louder now as Salazar loaded the next bucket of concrete to the mechanical spreader straddling the slab. "You gotta eagle eye each layer like a bartender. Fill a paving form half full, lay wire mesh over it because God forbid it cools too quickly and cracks. Add the next layer then smooth it with a screed to pop any last air bubbles. Why, Padre?"

"'Because God forbid it cools too quickly and cracks,'" Vilmos recited, grabbing a rake to disperse the concrete pouring out of the spreader.

Individual sections of highway were thirty-four feet wide to accommodate two ten-foot lanes of traffic, a passing lane, and two shoulders and twelve feet long. Each section was first blocked out by heavy steel forms that were then filled with concrete. After the slab was smoothed and left to cool, the forms would be laid for the next section following the route mapped months earlier by the surveyors and cleared by the demolition team. The paving crew's cement mixer would drive forward a few yards as the spreader was rolled down the steel forms to start the process over again with more buckets of concrete.

It was tedious, mind-numbing work in the best of times. The blistering heat of California's Mojave Desert where temperatures often rose above 100 degrees added several degrees of difficulty, making it downright onerous.

Vilmos eyed the waiting section and added another twelve feet to his running tally. They were 14 miles, 780 yards, and 2 feet northeast of Barstow with another 16 miles, 62 yards, and 8 feet of highway to pour before they reached Victorville. But they were only one part of a much bigger project to replace worn-out Route 66 with a brand-new, high-speed interstate connecting Los Angeles to Las Vegas.

#

Vilmos had never been to Vegas, but Watkins couldn't shut up about it, saying he'd seen everyone from Frank Sinatra to Ella Fitzgerald there. He even claimed to have shaken hands with Bing Crosby at the Sands and offered a joke to Liberace who later used it in his act.

Every squad and crew had a Watkins.

"After all that, you've gotta turn a hose on concrete to make sure it dries real slow," Watkins droned on. "Then you wrap it in paper like a Christmas present to block the sun. You know how long it'll take to cure Hoover Dam?"

125 years, thought Vilmos.

"125 years! Now, with *asphalt*—"

"My God, shut it, Watkins!"

Detmer, the paving crew supervisor, wandered over, golf bag slung over his shoulder. Though his job was to oversee the very process Watkins was describing, he spent his mornings chipping golf balls deep into the desert from the hood of his Army surplus Jeep.

"Asphalt is for neighborhood streets where Johnny plays ball and wifey drives her Buick to the butcher shop once a day," Detmer said, slow rotating his gold Princeton class ring around his finger. "Concrete is for heavy traffic and big weight. Trucks. Construction equipment. Fleets of cars. Tanks, if the Reds ever invade from the Pacific. Asphalt in a desert? It wouldn't last three years in this sun. Maybe four."

Watkins scoffed so loudly that even the fifth and final member of the paving crew, Carlyle, who drove the mixer and maintained the concrete, chuckled soundlessly by the mixer barrel. Soundlessly, because his voice had been slashed away with half his throat by a trench knife on Guadalcanal. He hid the wide scar behind a blue bandana that occasionally slipped down, revealing the mottled flesh that wrapped almost all the way around his neck. It was so gnarled, Vilmos thought it looked more like overlapping burn tissue than anything a blade could cause.

"Eh, who wants to go to Vegas anyway, man?" Watkins asked. "New Orleans! Now, that's the place to be!"

"Both are indistinguishable dens of vice," Detmer shot back. "And pardon me, Padre, but God does not approve vice, correct?"

Everyone eyed Vilmos, who never failed to regret revealing that he'd been a priest at one point and a chaplain during Korea, to see how he'd answer.

"I am in this hell with you idiots precisely because God no longer seems to think I am worthy of knowing what He does or does not approve of," Vilmos said, shrugging. "Ask someone else."

He didn't mean it to come out as sardonically as it did. Luckily, everyone just laughed. Until Carlyle urgently banged his wrench on the mixer and pointed north.

A great plume of dust rose from the unpaved farm track running parallel to the unfinished highway. The vehicle or vehicles kicking it up moved much faster than the paving crew's supply trucks or the chuck wagon. Besides, they rolled up the recently completed sections of highway when making their thrice-daily deliveries of food, water, cement, and gravel.

Vilmos spotted a car door painted with an arrowhead overlaying a six-pointed star. It was the symbol of the San Bernardino County Sheriff's Department. There were four cars in all, Chevy Bel-Airs, their red roof lights blinking on and off as they drove.

"Uh-oh," Watkins said.

"Finally," Detmer added.

"Guess it's bye-bye to the Master of the House," Salazar quipped.

Everyone looked east. The demolition team that had been stalled out about a hundred yards ahead of the paving crew whooped and yelled. They'd spent the last three days knocking down the last remaining buildings in a long-forgotten ghost town called Rio Rico to make way for the highway. They hauled all the remains away except for the foundation of one last house on the far side of town. Their path was blocked by an old man who was missing both legs, an arm, several teeth, and who sat alone in a rocking chair all day.

They tried to get him to move, cycling through legal jargon about eminent domain, offering money and rides, and even making threats. He refused, however, babbling on about how they would upset the "Master of the House." They assumed he was referring to himself, so the crews started calling him that.

As the Bel-Airs rolled past the demolition team on their way to the old man, Vilmos offered up a brief prayer. Not to the God who had long since turned away from him, but to the chaotic and disordered Universe itself.

Take pity on him, Vilmos prayed emptily. *Protect him from what's coming.*

Even as the words formed in his mind, he knew the prayer would go unanswered.

#

Vilmos was born in Hungary in 1925 near an orchard. Fifteen years later, he watched the Nazis hang his father in that very orchard for being a member of the outlawed Hungarian Communist Party. They'd saved Vilmos's dad for last, forcing him to watch his five confederates hang first, including his wife, for daring to resist their interrogation. To add insult to injury, they also strung him up with a short noose so he'd strangle rather than break his neck.

They also forced Vilmos to watch, his eyes locking with his father's for the twelve minutes it took for the older man's soul to leave his body. A neighbor eventually came to take him away, bundling Vilmos off to a Catholic seminary. He spent the rest of the war training for the priesthood. He was ordained a priest at war's end then immediately fled Hungary's postwar privation for America where he enlisted in the Army's chaplain corps. A few years later, he served in the Korean War.

He didn't know when he'd lost his faith. Plenty of his fellow chaplains lost theirs in the face of untold atrocities in war. He hated to think he was just one more who'd failed this test. But at some point when trapped on the western side of the Chosin Reservoir as his division suffered a 90-percent casualty rate over three days of bitterly cold combat, he realized the presence of God he'd felt since he was a child was gone. He prayed for it to return. To hear God's voice, the quietest of the many intruding on his thoughts, again.

It remained absent.

He spoke to other priests who'd endured God's silence, but they all had the same prescription: pray and listen. Don't put Him to the test. He gives us no burden greater than the one He gave his own son.

It was after he read St. John of the Cross's treatises on recovering from spiritual doubt that he knew he would have to leave the church behind.

I remained, lost in Oblivion.

He thought it was all of these things from his past that made him sympathize with the Master of the House. In Hungary, he'd watched uniformed officials throw people out of their homes and confiscate their property, citing some authority of the state. He saw it again in Los Angeles when entire neighborhoods (always poor, never white) were razed to make way for highways or even a western home for the Brooklyn Dodgers.

Now, he saw it as the Master of the House was being asked to leave what could well be the only home he knew.

The surveyors had warned the demolition team leader, Lanegan. They thought he might be part of a group intent on sabotaging the highway. Instead, he resisted in the only effective way he could. By refusing to move.

Once it was clear he couldn't be bought off, Detmer sent Vilmos to talk to him, likely hoping there was enough priest left in the young Hungarian to make a difference.

"You'll anger the Master of the House," the man in the old rocking chair had told Vilmos as the ex-priest looked over his crude amputations. "Do not defile this ground."

"They'll send police," Vilmos warned. "Let me take you to a motel. Is there someone I can call or write?"

"You'll anger the Master of the House," the sunbaked old man said, tongue lolling over broken teeth. "Do not defile this ground."

Vilmos left the man food and returned to the paving crew. When he checked on the man at dusk, the food hadn't been touched. The old man waggled his stumps at Vilmos.

"You'll anger the Master of the House," he said. "Do not defile this ground."

#

"San Berdoo sheriffs are real head breakers," Watkins said as the Bel-Airs reached their destination. "They're gonna make a fortune ticketing folks on this road. No way they'll let some old man get in the way."

Detmer plucked his binoculars from the Jeep and climbed on top of the cement mixer to watch the action.

"The deputies are out of their cars," he reported. "They are standing around the old man and talking down to him."

140

"What're they doing now?" Salazar asked, shading his eyes.

"One put a hand on the man's shoulder," Detmer said. "Ach, he batted it away."

Vilmos closed his eyes.

You'll anger the Master of the House. Do not defile this ground.

"They're taking out their nightsticks," Detmer said. "Oh. Oh, God."

It didn't matter how far away the deputies were. The desert was flat. The crack of the first blow echoed over the sound like a gunshot. There a second. Then a third. Then a fourth and fifth. Detmer lowered his binoculars and climbed off the mixer. Everyone slowly returned to work, even as the blows continued.

The Bel-Airs retreated half an hour later.

#

"All yours," Lanegan said from the cab of his dump truck, the demo team stopping by on their way back to base camp. "Bad business today."

Each of the four dump trucks was filled with the broken foundation of the house where the man in the rocking chair had sat vigil.

"Surely," Detmer replied. "Any word on his condition?"

Lanegan sighed and lowered his red steel helmet over his eyes.

"He's in the hospital," Lanegan said. "All we know."

The demo team drove off into the afternoon sun. A silence enveloped the paving crew, broken only when Vilmos took hold of a screed and hastily smoothed the most recently poured concrete. The others settled back into their tasks, but Vilmos worked like a man possessed. He increased the pace, spreading the incoming layers of concrete so quickly that Salazar had to hurry to keep full buckets pouring through the mechanical spreader.

"Where's the fire?" Watkins asked.

Vilmos didn't answer.

Carlyle added more cement, gravel, and water to the mixer barrel to keep up with demand. Salazar laid the forms for the next section and rolled the spreader over it. It was an hour later when they reached the remains of Rio Rico, and everyone seemed to realize the root of Vilmos's urgency. If there had been any lingering question, the sight of the old man's shattered rocking chair a couple dozen yards ahead in the desert hammered it home.

They needed to put this cursed site in their rear view as soon as possible.

The four men worked faster than they had on the entire job thus far, save Detmer, who snoozed in his Jeep. They connected the metal forms until they stretched over the desert like a lengthening bedframe. They spread concrete in each section, one layer at a time, then smoothed it flat before moving on.

The trucks from base camp arrived in the late afternoon with supplies, the grim visages of their drivers letting the paving crew know the story of the man in the rocking chair. It wasn't until the chuck wagon arrived with the evening meal that they got the news.

"The old man passed," the cook told Salazar. "Died in the backseat of one of their cars. Didn't even make it to Victorville."

Vilmos whispered his second prayer of the day. For the first time in a while, he longed for his connection with God. Wished he could still believe He was there. But it was so much easier to understand that the Universe, which meted out cruelties without malice or intention, had no more interest in his prayers than it did the weather.

It was well into the night, the headlights of the mixer and now Detmer's Jeep lighting the last sections, when Salazar pointed into the near desert.

"There it is," he said.

The rocking chair had been reduced to a pile of broken splinters. It wasn't hard to imagine what had been done to the old man. The men turned their focus back to burying the last remnants of Rio Rico beneath layers and layers of concrete.

#

To get an early start the next morning, the paving crew often camped out on the job site. Detmer slept in his Jeep. Watkins and Carlyle shared the cab of the mixer. Salazar, despite waking up once with a snake in his bed roll and another with a coyote looking him in the eye, preferred the open ground. Vilmos slept on the highway, still hot from the day's sun.

When he'd come back from Korea, he'd noticed that he not only preferred the heat, he practically required it. There were days, even at the height of summer, where he couldn't get warm enough. He'd met other veterans, included an ex-Marine, now-bricklayer, who had the same problem.

"The cold burrows in deep over there," the bricklayer told Vilmos while building a retaining wall next to a stretch of highway that had recently been the LA neighborhood of Rose Hill. "I've chased the sun all the way to the equator and back and still can't seem to stay warm."

Vilmos knew the feeling. In the desert, he was only comfortable at 90 degrees or higher. Over 100, he was in paradise. On those rare days that it pushed higher than 110 and the others knocked off to hide on the shady side of the mixer, Vilmos did the work of two.

At night, the desert temperature dropped into the fifties. Vilmos layered on the blankets, but his teeth still chattered as if he had a fever. He put on a jacket and wore his boots. It didn't matter. He could never stay warm.

The night of the man in the rocking chair's death, however, it was other matters that kept him awake. Vilmos gazed up into the night sky, eyes flitting from the sliver of a new moon to the constellations; he didn't know the name of a single one.

Who was the dead man to him? Nobody. How many people had he seen die meaningless deaths, ending their inconsequential lives in a blurry second or two of confused yet sanctioned violence? Dozens, up close. Hundreds, removed. So, why was he so disturbed by the grim demise of this old man who was likely only months from his natural death?

If there was a God, maybe there was a chance that justice would be done. But in His absence, there would be nothing at all. His killers were likely enjoying a beer at a Victorville bar right now or having dinner with their families, content they had done their duty.

Vilmos exhaled. And glimpsed movement in his peripheral vision.

They were accustomed to seeing wildlife—coyotes, jackrabbits, javelinas, even the occasional antelope. This was something different.

"Salazar?" he asked the night.

He'd said the spreader man's name because the figure he'd spied out in the dark desert was short. Just, much shorter than Salazar. In fact, it had the stubby arms and legs of a toddler. Lit only by faint moonlight, Vilmos wondered if it could be a child.

"Hey, you okay?"

The figure stopped moving. Vilmos wondered if it had been moving at all. He could be staring at a small cactus or old tree. The figure's silhouette was hazy and gray. It grew wider as if its torso was expanding over its limbs like a balloon.

It reminded Vilmos of snow blindness—when the horizon line vanished and you lost the ability to judge distance. How many times had he seen soldiers draw down on some mysterious figure in the snow-choked mountains, only to shoot snow and give away their positions?

This shape, however, faded into the background as if evaporating into the night, then reappeared on the other side of the highway. It was closer now.

Vilmos blinked, figuring something was wrong with his eyes. Nothing human could've moved that quickly. The figure remained frustratingly corporeal.

"Hey," Vilmos said, advancing toward it.

It didn't move. As he neared, something solid did come into view. A few more steps and Vilmos saw what it was.

The dead man's splintered rocking chair.

He sighed and returned to his bed roll on the highway. He didn't believe in God anymore. He sure as hell wasn't going to replace that with believing in ghosts.

#

"Where's the chuck wagon?" Watkins asked early the next morning. "I'm starving!"

The men had risen before dawn to make coffee, as usual. The chuck wagon usually arrived by five, and the resupply trucks not long after. Judging by the sun, they were over an hour later.

"Must be some kind of hold up," Detmer snapped. "If you hadn't worked into the night, maybe we'd have enough materials to start the day."

Carlyle tapped on the side of the tanker with his wrench. It thudded rather than clanged, indicating a full tank. Salazar ducked into the trailer and pulled out a couple of forty-pound sacks of cement.

"Oh, we got enough to get started," the spreader operator announced.

"Without breakfast?" Watkins complained.

"I will cook!" Detmer said, unlocking a footlocker in the back of the Jeep. "We have plenty of rations."

No one expected much, but Detmer quickly whipped up a hot breakfast of grits, powdered eggs with garlic salt, and pancakes. After another pot of coffee, all complaints evaporated.

"Can we get to work now?" Detmer asked.

Watkins and Vilmos lowered forms onto the desert to frame the next slab. Salazar rolled the spreader to the center as Carlyle prepped the concrete. When the first batch was ready, Salazar attached the bucket lines to the mixer, walked the empty bucket up to the discharge chute, and filled it up. Now weighing almost a hundred pounds, Salazar guided the full bucket back down the lines to attach it to the spreader.

He pulled a lever and concrete sluiced out through the nozzles into the empty form. Watkins and Vilmos used rakes to spread it evenly out to the edges.

And a new day of work was underway.

"I'll radio base camp and see what the holdup is," Detmer said, once the first layer was poured.

Everyone laughed. The radio seldom worked on the best of days. That Detmer had no real idea how to use it anyway was an open secret. Detmer tried the radio a few times but received only the expected static.

Watkins looked ready to complain, until Detmer let them break for lunch early after raiding the rations lockers a second time to make sandwiches on sourdough bread paired with another round of coffee.

When the sun slipped down toward the western horizon that evening, Carlyle banged the side of the mixer approvingly. They'd pulled off the impossible by stretching their supplies a full day, pouring 25 slabs for exactly 300 feet of concrete. A whole football field.

"Guess our supplies can go a lot longer than we thought," Detmer declared.

"One of the earlier sections must have cracked," Salazar said. "We didn't even see the demo team ride by. Bet they send someone up tomorrow telling us we have to backtrack."

This elicited groans. Vilmos went to the trailer to grab his bed roll but was caught up short by something in the desert. Only a few yards from the end of the new section of highway were the splintered remains of the old man's rocking chair.

He looked back down the hundred yards of concrete to where it had sat the night before. Had someone moved it? Brought it with them as a reminder? Impossible. It would've fallen apart. And he couldn't have walked all this way last night, could he have?

He decided questions could wait until morning and grabbed his bed roll, gazing back only one more time at the broken chair, glowing a dull gray in the dim light of the new moon.

#

The trucks didn't come the next morning, either. Detmer made coffee and pancakes and then tried the radio.

"Base camp, this is paving crew, come in, over," he said, more annoyance in his voice than urgency. "Base camp, this is Detmer, please respond, over."

The only response was static.

"Supplies or no supplies, you know they're going to dock our pay if we're out here and not working," Salazar said. "This needs to get fixed. Pronto."

"How much water do we have left?" Detmer asked.

"Enough for now," Watkins said, peering into the tank. "It'll go fast once the day heats up."

But Vilmos caught a glimpse of confusion on Carlyle's silent visage. Like things weren't quite adding up. He shared the feeling. As if something uncanny was going on, but he couldn't quite put his finger on it yet.

The supply trucks didn't show up any time that day, either.

Nor did the chuck wagon.

But the supplies didn't run out.

And for the third night in a row, the new moon rose in the east, gently illuminating the splintered rocking chair that again rested a few yards off in the desert alongside the day's last finished slab.

#

It was the moon that bothered Vilmos most of all.

"You're the one who has to keep the routine," his captain had once told him. "It's easy on the frontlines to become detached from the world. The date, the days of the week, they become unimportant, so you forget about them. Other things fall away. The boys stop thinking about getting home. That leads to despair. You have to be their connection. When they ask you the time, you tell them, Padre."

Vilmos had understood. He kept two watches in case one broke. Both did.

So, he learned about the phases of the moon. About its seasonal apex. How to determine moonrise and moonset. Even the lunar perigee and apogee.

All this told him that he couldn't possibly be staring up into a third new moon in as many nights. Where was the sliver of crescent-shaped light telling him that time had advanced? That the moon had continued its orbit around the earth and the earth around the sun?

He didn't want to tell the others for fear they'd think he was going mad in the heat. But those seemed to be the choices. He was either crazy or there was some sort of cosmic interruption to their activities here in the desert.

My God, he scoffed to himself.

What if it is the latter?

What then?

He scoffed a second time and closed his eyes, soon falling into the deepest sleep he'd had in months.

#

No trucks arrived on the third morning. There was no breakfast awaiting the men, either.

"Where's Detmer?" Salazar asked, checking the supervisor's Jeep.

Everyone turned to the desert.

"There," Vilmos said, pointing out toward the fire road.

Detmer stood alone, turning first one way then the other, barely visible in the predawn light. The men trooped over to him, the hardpacked sand turning loose and hard to traverse the further they got from the unfinished highway.

"What're you looking at, Detmer?" Watkins asked. "Think the trucks'll come up the fire road?"

Detmer didn't speak for a moment. He turned his Princeton class ring over and over on his finger.

"I saw him last night," Detmer said. "He was right here. But there are no tracks."

"Who'd you see?" Salazar asked. "Someone from base camp?"

"A man," Detmer said. "Or a demon. He's been watching us. He's the one moving the chair."

Vilmos straightened. So, he wasn't the only one who'd noticed.

"Maybe it's time we drove down to base camp," Salazar said. "Between the Jeep and the mixer, we should all get there in half an hour or so. We could even walk."

"No!" Detmer cried, staring back at the highway. "We are not to leave. *I* am not to leave. He has condemned us to this place. We are bound here."

"What're you talking about?" Watkins asked, rolling his eyes. "Are you scared of something out there on the sand?"

"You're not?" Salazar asked. "Or are we going to keep pretending the water tank isn't refilling itself? That the mixer is bottomless? Or that each day we start from the same position as if our day's work was undone during the night?"

Vilmos hadn't thought to mark their beginning spot. He wondered what else the others had noticed.

"You don't know what's out there," Detmer said. "He came to me in the darkness. Watched over me like a ghost."

"You're crazy," Watkins said.

"He came to me, too," Vilmos said. "It's how Detmer describes it. A small man. Vanished into the ether when I approached."

"Really?" Salazar asked. "Thought you were a non-believer."

"He's out there," Detmer warned, pointing toward base camp. "He won't let us leave."

"So, it's slavery?" Salazar asked. "Not what I signed up for."

"All right," Watkins said. "Why don't you drive down to base camp and tell us what you find."

Salazar glared at Watkins but didn't move. No one did.

"I'll go," Vilmos said.

Salazar sneered. Watkins looked perplexed.

"No, you don't have to go, Padre," Watkins said. "They'll be along in a minute to sort all this out."

"No, they won't," Detmer said.

"You hush," Watkins said. "Got enough out of you this morning. Padre, you stay here with us."

"No, one of us has to go," Vilmos said. "It can be me."

This time, no one protested.

Vilmos unloaded the rations footlockers from the Jeep and climbed behind the wheel. Carlyle tapped his shoulder and handed him a slip of paper.

It read: *Stay on the highway.*

Vilmos nodded, wondering what Carlyle knew, and started the Jeep. He drove it onto the finished section of highway, waved to the men, and headed toward base camp. Within minutes, the paving crew disappeared in his rear view. He was soon alone.

The desert passed anonymously on both sides. There were mesas on the northern horizon but few and too far away to mark distances. There were cacti and tumbleweeds, but little else.

Base camp was a mile north of Victorville. Made up of a few tents, some large, some small, it primarily served as a supply depot to run materials out to the paving and demolition crews though all the crews took refuge there during a sandstorm.

Salazar was right. In theory, it should've taken Vilmos half an hour or even less to get there. After an hour of driving, he knew this wasn't to be.

Not that he knew it was an hour. The Jeep's clock had stopped advancing. The sun still hung in the same position as when he'd left the paving crew. The gas needle hadn't gone down nor had the odometer rolled.

He pressed. His legs never grew tired. His back never grew stiff.

His eyes never dried out. He wished for food or water for the distraction, though he was never hungry. He counted time, marking minutes against speed to calculate how far he'd gone.

After a couple of hours, he figured he should be in Los Angeles. Later, the Pacific Ocean. He considered driving off into the sand, but Carlyle's warning prevented him. If Salazar and Detmer knew more about what was going on, why not Carlyle?

Something new appeared up ahead. At first, Vilmos thought he was looking at a mirage. Shadows in the heat lines. As he drew near, he saw that there were four dump trucks pulled just off the highway. He slowed the Jeep, easing up to them at a crawl.

It was the demolition team. Their vehicles, at least. They'd been parked there so long they were half-buried in sand. Their hulls had rusted through from sporadic rainfall.

Vilmos parked the Jeep and checked each truck. He expected to find them empty. To his surprise, there were indications that Lanegan and his men had been here for some time.

Steering wheels had been removed and seats converted to beds. There were improvised camp stoves and water collection devices. There was a pair of work boots, the soles of which had been worn down from what looked like miles of walking.

He looked under the trucks. There was nothing there. He climbed over the rusty tailgates of the lead truck and saw the broken remains of the last house in Rio Rico.

Something glinted in the near desert.

He hurried over to it. Half-buried in the desert sand was a large circle filled with sculptural designs. There were flat geometric shapes with tiny figures made of sticks. There were also individual pieces that resembled an octopus's garden of tiny stones.

Except the stones were teeth.

The figures were made from ribcages.

And the flat shapes: everything from smashed skulls to bits of leathered flesh hanging off crumbling femurs and skulls.

He'd found Lanegan's men.

In the center was a mostly complete skeleton, a broken piece of mirror still in its hand. Its feet and hands were bound in decaying cloth. When Vilmos looked under the bindings, he found missing toes and fingers, the bones around them chipped and gashed.

He wondered if this could've been done by animals, but the cuts were too deep. This could've only been done by an edged weapon. He checked the other bones in the circle. These were also covered in tell-tale gashes.

Only, many of these looked fatal. Chiseled eye sockets. Splintered ribs and breast bones. Crushed kneecaps and snapped tibias. The men had been killed and dismembered. Vilmos wasn't sure which came first.

He returned to the man with the broken mirror. Could it have been Lanegan? One of the others? He didn't know. Whoever he was, he seemed to be the author of his own amputations.

Did he kill all the others first? Vilmos wondered.

And why the ritualistic arrangement?

What god was he trying to appease?

#

"Jesus Christ!" came a shout. "It's Vilmos!"

Vilmos snapped out of his reverie. After finding the demo team, he'd climbed back into the Jeep and drove on toward base camp. Or so he'd thought. Up ahead of him was his own team coming out to greet him. He was no longer on finished highway but packed sand.

Had he turned around at some point?

No, if that had been the case, he'd have approached the paving crew from the west on finished highway. Instead, he was coming from the east as if he'd driven in a great loop.

Salazar raced the short distance from the end of the finished section of highway to the Jeep. Watkins was right behind him. Carlyle hopped out of the mixer and brought up the rear.

There was no sign of Detmer.

"It's you!" Salazar bellowed. "I can't believe it!"

It wasn't until Vilmos had stopped the Jeep and climbed out that he got a good look at the three men. Carlyle and Watkins appeared very much the same as when Vilmos had left. Salazar was virtually unrecognizable. He looked smaller. His eyes had shrunken back into his skull. The skin around his face was loose. He looked weathered and even ran with a slight stoop. It looked as if he'd aged several years.

"Padre!" Watkins said, throwing his arms around Vilmos. "We thought you were dead."

"I've only been gone a few hours," Vilmos said. "At most."

Watkins laughed then stopped himself as if realizing Vilmos wasn't kidding. He shot a glance to Carlyle then put a hand on Vilmos's shoulder.

"We understand that's what you believe," Watkins said. "But I need you to take a look at yourself."

Watkins indicated the Jeep's side view mirror. Vilmos stared at the old man's visage gazing back at him. It was like some kind of trick. He'd lost hair. His eyes were wet and rheumy. His skin was as loose and leathered as Salazar's. He ran his hand over his face. He waited to feel horror or revulsion. Even fear. Sorrow.

Instead, he recognized something he thought he'd never feel again—the presence of the divine. Not himself, but whoever had authored this strange transformation.

"You don't surprise easily, eh, Padre?" Watkins asked. "When Salazar got back, we thought he'd just about lose his mind!"

Salazar scowled; Vilmos smiled. He felt lighthearted, as if a tremendous weight had been gently lifted from his shoulders.

He followed the men back to the shade of the mixer and told them about his journey, his observations about time and the Jeep, but also his discovery of the demo team's trucks. He left out the discovery of the bodies and his theory of what had happened. He didn't want to disrupt the jovial mood he'd inspired by his return.

"How long have I been gone?" Vilmos asked, wondering if it would correspond with how much he'd aged.

"We don't know," Watkins said. "Twelve years? Fifteen? Twenty? We're unable to keep track."

"And you didn't age in any of that time?" Vilmos asked.

"Only by mistake," Watkins said.

"What do you mean?"

"As long as we do what we're meant to do," Salazar interjected, pointing to the unfinished highway, "we do not age. We build and rebuild it, day in and day out. Sunup to sundown."

"My God," Vilmos said. "And you don't age a day?"

"We tested it," Watkins said. "Went slow some days, knocked off altogether on others to build shelters. That caught up to us. We'd age several months over just a couple of days. We didn't know what had happened until Carlyle suggested we get back to it."

"But what is causing it?" Vilmos asked, though he thought he knew the answer. "Is it a natural phenomenon?"

"The Master of the House," Watkins said.

"That man in the rocking chair?"

"No, we no longer think he was referring to himself," Watkins explained, Vilmos realizing a determined calm had settled over the man in the intervening years. "We think he was referring to the being both you and Detmer mentioned seeing in the desert. The being we have all seen now. The small god of this place. The *duende* or dueño de casa."

Salazar, appearing annoyed by this, rose to head off.

"*Duende*?" Vilmos asked.

"I remembered this one day," Watkins admitted. "Took me long enough. I had a neighbor in New Orleans who believed in *duende*. Also called them *tomtes*. Said they were like a leprechaun but extremely powerful. They're like household gods but tied to a single dwelling."

"A genie in a lamp?" Vilmos said.

"Something like that," Watkins continued. "They cause mischief in the house. A broken plate, missing keys. But they also protect it. If they're freed, it's a different story. They're said to lure children into the woods. Send travelers down endless roads who wander forever, never to be found. Sound familiar?"

The small god of this place. Vilmos looked to Carlyle. The big man nodded.

Salazar slapped the side of the water tank in disgust. "See why I took off, too?" he asked. "When people start believing in leprechauns and fairies, I can't hang around."

"But you came back," Vilmos said.

"Not by choice," Salazar said. "Now, if you're done, maybe you'd like to hold back the aging for a little while longer by getting to work."

Vilmos hadn't even gotten a chance to ask about Detmer.

#

It took Vilmos a few days to adjust to the idea of laying concrete for a road that would only be torn up that night. It didn't make sense until, after hearing Watkins recite every way they tried to free themselves from the task, he understood it was the only way forward.

To pass the time, they sang every song they knew and recited the plots of books and movies. Watkins knew *Snow White* by heart. Salazar knew *The Wizard of Oz*. They discussed radio serials as if they were myths. They told stories of their own ancestry like tall tales.

At one point, Vilmos came to understand that Watkins and Carlyle had had an intimate relationship at one time, but it was now in the distant past. He felt his age as he worked. There was pain in his legs and back. His body was no longer that of a young man.

Still, in quiet moments, he reveled in the mystery of his evolution. He knew there was horror and madness here. The demolition team had been driven to violence and were all dead. Detmer, who he'd finally asked Carlyle about, had simply wandered off one night never to return. They assumed he was dead, too. All of this had begun with an act of savagery that had ushered them into a kind of purgatory.

It didn't matter. Vilmos felt restored by the presence of this god every minute of every day. It was a feeling he'd craved his whole life, one he now thought he'd imagined or feigned in seminary. But it was real now. This god, this *duende*, not only held his life in his hands, but also the universe. The recurring new moon. The arrangement of stars. He wondered if the whole galaxy was born from this barely seen creature.

Somehow, he doubted it. He didn't mind "a god of small things."

Vilmos rose each day to take his morning meals with the others, surprised no one remarked on who provided them. For reasons he could only define as genuine gratitude, he began whispering a prayer of thanks before each meal.

"Thank you, *duende*," he'd say. "Thank you, *tomte*. Thank you, Master."

At first, he kept it to himself, but it was difficult. After losing his faith so many years before, he would still publicly go through the motions of fealty and ritual, whether in celebrating a Mass or delivering a blessing. No one expected a priest to fake it, so no one realized he was false.

But now, he felt a strange zeal. He *was* grateful for the day. For the meal. For the work. For the fellowship of others. For the warmth. For the night.

"Thank you, *duende*," he whispered. "Thank you, *tomte*. Thank you, Master."

#

One night, Carlyle pressed a note into Vilmos's hand.

To whom do you pray? Thought you'd left your belief in God behind.

"To our provider, the god of this place," Vilmos said. "To the Master of the House."

Carlyle stared at him like he'd gone mad. Vilmos shrugged.

"I'm not here to proselytize," Vilmos said. "It is for me alone. I'm not a priest anymore."

To his surprise, a few days later, Vilmos watched as Carlyle mouthed the prayer as well. Two days after that, Watkins whispered it as well.

Vilmos did not believe the Master craved their prayers. Doubted he even listened to them. But as he told Carlyle, it was for his own edification. He found it uplifting.

Thank you, *duende*. Thank you, *tomte*. Thank you, Master.

Salazar said nothing.

#

"The last time I prayed, it was for death," Watkins said one night as they gathered around a fire. "I wanted to die, but I couldn't bring myself to do it. I have a wife and a son. I still hope to see them again one day."

Vilmos nodded. He knew Carlyle had a wife, too. Salazar had often spoken of his four children, though he didn't anymore. Even Detmer had a fiancée.

"But I don't know if that's reason enough to keep going," Watkins said. "After all this time, I mean. Why do this every day, maybe forever?"

The former seminarian in Vilmos winced. It was like an old question between priests. What do you tell a man in Hell? How do you give hope to someone who has lost the will to live? In Hungary, there was the belief the Nazis would one day leave. In Korea, that the Army would go home. But here?

"There are rules here which suggests a plan," Vilmos said carefully. "But by its very design, we are not allowed to understand it. Our preservation comes from obedience. We must have faith that there is redemption."

Is this a punishment? Carlyle wrote on a scrap of paper. *For what was done to the man in the rocking chair?*

157

"I don't know," Vilmos said. "But if there is a cause, if there is a beginning, it's logical to believe there could be an end."

"Y'all have stumbled upon a new level of insanity," Salazar quipped. "You're like baseball fans or political boosters. You *need* something to worship, or you don't know what to do with yourself. Even if it's a devil who serves as your jailer."

"Were we not warned?" Vilmos asked. "Didn't the old man in the rocking chair warn us not to defile this ground? Don't we share in the culpability?"

Salazar laughed. "Oh, so you're stirring Jesus and the Devil with this half-baked scrap of remembrance about some house leprechaun? If I pretend to believe in him, you think he'll bring me a pot of gold? You know nothing at all. You stumble through the dark forcing puzzle pieces to fit together then pat yourselves on the back all, 'Hallelujah, we've solved the mystery!' It's invention. It's preposterous."

After everyone turned in, Vilmos stayed up late into the night considering this. He thought about it the next day at work and into the following evening. He said little over the next week. It reminded him of why priests and monks made promises of silence. It removed the passive conversations that eased one through the day and forced a person to confront their own thoughts.

To confront God.

He focused first on their location. Why here? Because it was such an easy place to get lost? Or was this stretch of desert more sacred than they knew? He tried to remember everything he could about the man in the rocking chair. His voice. His words.

His missing limbs.

Missing limbs?

Vilmos opened his eyes. It was night now. He'd been asleep on the highway.

Had the man hacked off his own limbs like the fellow on the demolition team? What did it mean then that he was somehow allowed to live?

A sound from out in the night interrupted his thoughts. Vilmos recognized it immediately, the strange, hog-like snore of agonal breathing that meant a body was dying. He sat up straight in time to see the dim silhouette of a man slam a wrench onto the head of another man. The wet squish that followed told him that the wrench had broken through skull to churn brain.

"Stop!" Vilmos screamed. "You're killing him!"

The man holding the wrench turned. It was Salazar. He eyed Vilmos then fled into the darkness. Vilmos raced to the stricken man's side. Though his face was completely caved in, Vilmos could see it was Watkins.

"Why'd you lie, Padre?" Salazar whispered from somewhere in the night. "Why didn't you tell them the part about the demolition team being all torn apart like that? How they turned this into some kind of religion and were trying to appease their captor with sacrament?"

Vilmos blinked. So, Salazar had seen the demo team in his wanderings, too.

He heard movement behind him but turned too slow, his old man's reflexes failing him. Salazar struck Vilmos in the head with the wrench. Vilmos spun to the ground, blood drizzling from his shattered teeth and broken nose.

"Stop," Vilmos whispered, sand caking to his bleeding face. "We can figure this out. There are clues to his nature."

"You believe that," Salazar said, raising the wrench. "That's why you're dangerous."

Before he could bring it down, Carlyle flew out of the darkness. He tackled Salazar and brought him down onto the road. Hard. Vilmos expected a fight. Instead, he heard the dull crunch of a breaking spine.

Carlyle lumbered over and helped Vilmos to his feet. Together, they confirmed that Watkins was dead before returning to Salazar's body. He had a weak pulse, but that wouldn't last. Something glinted in the dead man's hand. Vilmos picked it up.

Detmer's class ring glinted back at him.

#

Do you think Salazar killed Detmer? Carlyle wrote on his pad the next morning after they'd buried the two men.

"Don't know," Vilmos said, laying out the forms which had been duly restocked during the night, on the desert floor.

Do you think we're being tested?

"Maybe," Vilmos said. "I do wonder something..."

Carlyle shot him a questioning look as he fired up the spreader.

"What if Salazar was right?" Vilmos asked. "About our invisible god demanding a sacrament?"

Carlyle scratched the wide scar around his neck as if annoyed he had no voice with which to jeer Vilmos.

"Wait, listen," Vilmos said. "What Watkins said about the Master of the House... what if it was the demolition of his house that freed him?"

Carlyle rolled his eyes.

"What if this thing is more like the gods of old? What did the Greeks believe their gods wanted made for them? The Egyptians?"

Carlyle hesitated, not knowing the answer.

"What if all we need to do is build the Master a new house?" Vilmos asked.

Carlyle scribbled onto a piece of paper.

You believe if we worship a false god properly, it will bestow a kindness on us?

"I don't know," Vilmos said. "But I'm not ready to give up or pretend this is unsolvable."

You want us to be free? Or you want to know the nature of God?

"Can't both things be true?" Vilmos asked.

What're you asking to do?

"Build it a house," Vilmos said. "But only at night. Never when we're meant to be on the highway."

Carlyle didn't reply. They didn't speak anymore that day. Vilmos knew his comrade was still mourning Watkins, the man he'd been partnered with for years and years longer than he had with Vilmos. But the next morning, Vilmos awoke to three simple drawings Carlyle had made showing how they could use their existing forms and concrete to make a small structure.

What if he doesn't resupply us?

Vilmos didn't have an answer for this.

They worked on the highway through the day, made dinner at dusk, then began executing Carlyle's plan. The "temple" was to be a small, rectangular building about twelve feet by six feet using a framework of forms. These would be stacked onto one another side by side to create a narrow space between an inner and outer wall. Concrete would be poured in the gap. Forms would be sawn off on one side to create a doorway. A roof would be made from the walls of the supply trailer. They hoped this offering would do.

Unfortunately, their construction skills were lacking. They couldn't finish by sunrise.

"We'll get back to it tonight," Vilmos suggested.

But during the day, the half-built temple vanished.

Guess he didn't like it, Carlyle wrote.

That night, they tried again but managed even less. They took the next night off after redoing their plans. On the third attempt, they almost finished, but couldn't get the roof right. The fourth time, however, they nailed it with time to spare.

It, too, vanished during the day.

But they never ran out of supplies.

Vilmos wracked his brain. Was this a test? Maybe their new god wanted a different temple built every night to prove their fealty? And for how long? Weeks? Months?

"We need to try again tonight," he said.

Carlyle was dubious, but they built a fifth temple. It was gone the next evening as well. They took a few nights off. Erected six in six nights.

They made them slightly larger then slightly smaller. They tried to consecrate them with blessings.

They were always gone.

Maybe it's not this duende after all, Carlyle wrote.

They kept building.

While working on a fifth temple in as many nights, Vilmos suddenly cut his hand while sawing the forms around the doorway, an act he'd done dozens of times now.

"Gah!" he cried.

It was a deep gash. Blood flowed down his hand and into the wet concrete. He found a cloth and wrapped it tight. He got back to work, finished the temple with time to spare, and rose to build the section of highway the next morning.

As they neared evening, they spotted something up ahead. It resembled a narrow, branchless tree trunk. They finished the required section of highway then walked out to it. To their surprise, it was a thin column of concrete. Rather than destroy the entire temple, the god had left behind a sliver of what they'd built the night before.

Vilmos studied it for a moment before realizing it was a part of the doorway. Visible in the concrete were threads of brown where his blood had been mixed in.

Why is this here? Carlyle wrote.

Vilmos knew right away.

"Where did we bury Watkins and Salazar again?" he asked.

Carlyle scrunched his brow then pointed to a spot in the desert. Vilmos's eyes traveled up to the gnarled scar around Carlyle's neck. He reached for his trowel and whispered a prayer.

"Thank you, *duende*. Thank you, *tomte*. Thank you, Master."

\#

I am free. But I am lost.

I am free. But I am lost.

"I am free. But I am lost."

The doors of the Flying J Truck Stop outside Primm, Nevada slid open. A middle-aged clerk with a nametag reading Mariela nodded at Vilmos seated on the concrete bench out front.

"Sir? Can I help you this morning?" she asked in a tone devoid of judgment.

Vilmos knew he looked like hell. What was left of his hair was long and tangled. His skin was as tanned and leathered as an old saddle. He couldn't smile without revealing more missing teeth than he could explain. He couldn't gesture with his right hand without showing off his three missing fingers, nor his left hand as his arm was missing up to his shoulder.

"I'm all right," Vilmos whispered, his voice such a pathetic rasp it made him snicker.

"Sure about that?" she asked, chuckling as well.

Vilmos laughed for real now. He stared straight ahead at the sun rising over the eastern horizon, not wanting to reveal the missing ear on the left side of his head.

"Yeah," he said. "Just catching my breath before the start of a new day."

It had been ninety-six days since he'd finished the temple and locked away his god, waking up alone to a finished highway and a perilous, uncertain present. Locked away his *duende*. His *tomte*. His Master. Ninety-six days with nothing but sand and squalor. Ninety-six days without higher purpose. Ninety-six days of dwindling strength and the indignities of age, his own thoughts becoming as slippery and elusive as quicksilver.

Ninety-six days of having the ability to do anything he desired except what he wanted to do most of all—feel the presence of the god who had looked away to shine his holy light anywhere but on him.

I remain, lost in Oblivion.

"Maybe this'll help," the clerk said, placing a cup of hot coffee on the bench. "What is that around your neck? Makes you look like a priest."

163

Vilmos touched the wide strip of gnarled leather around his neck, the improvised necklace looking more like burn tissue than the scarred skin from a knife wound, save the nick at the end where Vilmos had finished the job a Japanese soldier had begun so many decades before.

"He was a friend," Vilmos said idly.

The clerk seemed unsure how to interpret this.

"It's slow right now if you want to use the showers," she offered, nodding into the station. "I can give you tokens for the laundry, too. Just don't go stealing nothing."

Vilmos had been inside the truck stop. He'd seen it from the desert all lit up like a carnival. The night clerk hadn't been as nice as this woman. Given his appearance, he couldn't blame him. He'd walked around the brightly lit interior in a daze, gazing in disbelief from a TV behind the counter through the aisles of food and drinks to the racks of gadgets and clothing. With difficulty, he'd used his remaining fingers to flip through a magazine, trying without success to absorb the words and images on every page.

It confirmed what he'd feared over the past several weeks as he made his way through the desert, encountering cars and trucks flying by at unheard of speeds. Seeing folks at rest stops in clothing as far removed from his frame of reference as suits of armor or powdered wigs. Even watching giant airplanes pass overhead.

"Two-thousand-twenty-three," he said.

"What's that?" the clerk asked.

"Two-thousand-twenty-three," Vilmos repeated, pointing to a rack of wall calendars near the register.

"Yep, 2023," she confirmed. "Is that news to you?"

It was, but Vilmos didn't think it'd have made much difference to him if it was 2043 or 2083. He'd been a man outside of time from the moment they'd torn down the Master's house.

He closed his eyes, wearied by the memory.

"You getting away from some place?" the clerk asked gently. "Or trying to get somewhere?"

It was the simplest of questions, but it brought tears to Vilmos's eyes.

"I'm looking for an unfinished stretch of highway," Vilmos replied, answering both questions at once. "Outside Rio Rico."

"Don't know it," Mariela said. "What's there?"

"The temple."

"The temple? You in a cult or something?"

"No, I erected it myself and then I was cast out," Vilmos replied, with irony. "I built it with my own hands."

His hands, but also his teeth, ears, toes, blood, as well as the bodies of his friends. A temple of carrion and concrete meant to set him free.

"Huh," the clerk said. "If that's the case, then maybe you should tear it down once you find it."

Vilmos knew she meant it as a joke. But the naïve truth of the statement struck him like a blow to the chest. What better way to once again become a servant than to desecrate something holy and beg for supplication?

A pickup truck with a pair of wildland fire fighters in the cab pulled up to the front of the truck stop.

"Morning, Mariela!" one of the fire fighters said, heading into the truck stop.

"Morning, Roy—fresh coffee awaits within," Mariela said, nodding to Vilmos as she rose to her feet. "Let me know if you want those laundry tokens."

Vilmos nodded, but he hadn't heard her. He stared at the equipment piled in the truck. Amidst the saws and picks was a heavy pry bar with an axe head on the other end. It looked like the kind of thing that could pull open a rusted door as easily as bring down a tree.

Or a temple.

The words of the old man in the rocking chair returned for the first time in years.

You'll anger the Master of the House. Do not defile this ground.

The old man had been wrong. Defiling the ground put one in the

Master's service. If you buckled at this, you would die, lost in the wastelands. But if you accepted it, accepted the glorious requirements of devotion and fidelity, you could live forever in the light, provided for, cared for, never to age a day. Devotion rewarded with devotion.

With a renewed sense of purpose, Vilmos got to his feet and moved to the pickup.

About the Authors

Matt Neil Hill lives in the UK with his wife, son, and the ghosts of cats. His horror/weird fiction has appeared in publications including *Vastarien, Cosmic Horror Monthly, Weirdbook, Mysterium Tremendum,* and the anthologies *Stories of the Eye* (Weirdpunk Books) and *Violent Vixens: An Homage to Grindhouse Horror* (Dark Peninsula Press). His essay on David Cronenberg's *The Lie Chair* was featured in *Children of the New Flesh* (11:11 Press). You can find him on Bluesky as @mattneilhill.bsky.social and, assuming it still exists, on Twitter as @mattneilhill.

Scott McCloskey, author of "Purgatory's Paradise," is a father, novelist, tabletop gamer, and dog show roadie to the love of his life. He has dabbled in several aspects of fiction writing, including commission work, fanfiction, and adaptation for audio/comic books. As a student of multiple genres, Scott's typewriter sometimes emits YA adventure fiction by day, but is subject to occasional fits of lycanthropy, and is known to go bump in the backwoods Pennsylvanian night. Scott's work has been featured in publications such as *Paying the Ferryman* by Charon Coin Press and Horror Bound magazine. His full-length pieces are available on Amazon. Scott maintains a book review blog catering to indie press and/or self-published authors at his personal website, RainHand Books. Yes, he wants to read your story.

Scotty Milder, author of "Twelve Miles. Two Hours.," was born and raised in Los Alamos, New Mexico, the birthplace of the atomic bomb. He began publishing short stories in indie horror magazines while in college, and went on to earn an MFA in Screenwriting from Boston University. He has developed screenplays with independent producers and major Hollywood studios, and his low-budget feature film *Dead Billy* is available on Amazon, Google Play, and other streaming platforms. His short fiction has appeared or will appear in Dark Matter Magazine, Cosmic Horror Monthly, the Scare You To Sleep podcast, and anthologies from Dark Moon Books, HellBound Books, Sinister Smile Press, Dark Ink Books, and others. He is also the creator and host of the Horror from the High Desert podcast and co-host of The Weirdest Thing history podcast with actor/theatre artist Amelia Ampuero. You can follow him online at scottymilder.com.

S.R. Miller, author of "Unwanted," hails from the Midwest, but formative years playing Oregon Trail have led him to make the slow journey west, where he has somehow avoided dying of dysentery. Along with writing, his love of the arts has taken many forms, including playing guitar in heavy metal bands, and working with an indie game company. Author of the horror novel *Sweet Dreams for Laura*, he and his wife now call Oregon home. Follow him on Facebook at facebook.com/srmwriting.

Christi Nogle, author of "Lights Out, Everything Off," is the author of the Shirley Jackson Award nominated and Bram Stoker Award winning first novel *Beulah* (Cemetery Gates Media) and the short fiction collections *The Best of Our Past, the Worst of Our Future* and *Promise* (Flame Tree Press). She is co-editor with Willow Dawn Becker of the Bram Stoker Award nominated anthology *Mother: Tales of Love and Terror* (Weird Little Worlds) and co-editor with Ai Jiang of *Wilted Pages: An Anthology of Dark Academia* (Shortwave Publishing). Follow her at https://christinogle.com and on across social media @christinogle.

Canadian author **Mary Rajotte, author of "Last Frequency,"** has a penchant for penning nightmarish tales of Gothic folk horror, which have been published in a number of anthologies. In 2022, she launched Frightmarish: a quarterly Gothic LitZine for devotees of dark fiction, poetry and the creative macabre. Her debut dark paranormal fantasy novel, *The Bone Key,* will launch in Autumn 2024 from Quill & Crow Publishing House. When Mary isn't writing, you can find her standing on her tiptoes at concerts or conjuring ideas by moonlight. Sometimes camera-elusive but always coffee-fueled, Mary lives in Toronto, Canada with her fiancé. She welcomes messages via her website maryrajotte.com.

Darren Todd, author of "S.A.L.E.," is a freelance book editor for Evolved Publications, and his short fiction has appeared in more than forty publications over the years. He has had four plays and a feature-length film produced and a non-fiction book published. While some of his works fall under the literary umbrella, he often returns to genre. His style and reading preferences tend toward the psychological, as he enjoys stories that linger in the imagination long after he's closed the book on them. He lives in Asheville, North Carolina with his son and girlfriend. See what he's up to at darrentodd.net.

Little is known about horror author, **Charlotte Vale, author of "Riders on the Storm,"** except that she writes from somewhere in the Pacific Northwest, loves to travel, and is extremely protective of her privacy. Various theories have arisen regarding her uncanny ability to compose such vivid realism in her stories, but nothing conclusive has been verified at this time. Ms. Vale is rumored to keep a vast collection of knives, odd pieces of men's clothing, and other various objects locked securely in her basement, but no eyewitness has come forward to confirm this claim. For the foreseeable future, we may only get to know Ms. Vale through her stories, however, she can be contacted through fellow author, Rebecca Olmstead, at www.rebeccaolmstead.com.

Mark Wheaton, author of "Master of the House," got his start in horror writing for FANGORIA magazine before graduating to movies, novels, short stories, games, and comics. His most recent book, "Who Haunts You," arrived in 2023 from Off Limits Press.

About the Editor

Aric Sundquist is an author of speculative fiction and owner/editor of Dark Peninsula Press. Born and raised in Michigan's Upper Peninsula, he graduated from Northern Michigan University with a Master's Degree in Creative Writing. His short stories have appeared in numerous publications, including *The Best of Dark Moon Digest*, *Night Terrors III*, *Daylight Dims*, *Fearful Fathoms Vol 1*, and *Attic Toys*. A writer and a musician at heart, he also enjoys board games, guitar, and traveling. Currently, he lives in Marquette, Michigan, with his girlfriend Elsa, and a ferocious beagle named Bruce. You can visit his author website at aricsundquist.weebly.com.

Dark Peninsula Press
www.darkpeninsulapress.com

Anthologies:

Negative Space: An Anthology of Survival Horror

Negative Space 2: A Return to Survival Horror

Violent Vixens: An Homage to Grindhouse Horror

The Cellar Door (Anthology Series):

Woodland Terrors: The Cellar Door Issue #1

Forbidden Magic: The Cellar Door Issue #2

Dark Highways: The Cellar Door Issue #3

Novellas/Novelettes:

Serious Applicants Only: A Horror Comedy